Monster

Alycia Linwood

ISBN-13: 978-1508538356
ISBN-10: 1508538352

I dedicate this book to my awesome readers. Thank you for your support! A big thanks to my beta readers and editors. I don't know what I would do without you all!

Chapter 1

When my eyes opened again, the first thing I saw was the light blue sky. I blinked, sharp pain shooting through my head. It wasn't the sky that I was seeing. It was a ceiling. I slowly moved my head to the left, licking my dry, cracked lips. The metallic taste of blood seemed to be stuck to the back of my tongue. A machine stood next to the bed I was lying on, but it appeared to be turned off. An IV bag was hooked to my arm, and a wave of dread hit me when I noticed Elemontera's bracelet was gone from my wrist.

What had happened to me? Where was I? I tried to reach my elements, but there was only a strange numbness inside of me. Focusing on my surroundings, I strained my muscles in an attempt to lift myself up on my elbows, but my whole body was weak, tiny tremors running all over my legs and arms. As far as I could tell, I was in a small room with light blue walls that didn't resemble anything I'd seen in Elemontera. A chair stood in the corner, a small dark brown table in front of it.

The door swung open and my heart shot into my

throat. Two guards poked their heads inside, looking at me. Their uniforms were black and didn't have any symbols or marks.

"She's awake," one of the guards said, turning to someone who was probably standing in the hallway.

"Let me through!" my mom's voice rang loud and clear from the outside. "I swear, if you don't let me see my daughter right now..."

I breathed out a sigh of relief, glad that my mom was okay, and that I hadn't been taken by the enemy. But why wouldn't the guards—I assumed Lily's guards—let my mom see me?

"We don't know what your daughter's state of mind is right now." I recognized Lily's calm voice. "I know you want to see her, but she might be dangerous. All those people didn't just drop to the ground because they felt like it. You know what she's done. We can't just..."

My mom snorted in disgust. "I'm not afraid of my daughter! Step aside right now or I'm going to go through you."

"I agree with my wife," my dad said. "Either let us see her or we'll make you."

Someone sighed, probably Lily. "Okay, but be careful."

Gathering my strength, I pushed myself up, letting out a small groan of pain. Had a herd of elephants run me over recently or what? My mom and dad rushed into the room, their faces brightening when they saw me.

"Honey!" My mom pulled me into her arms, and my

dad squeezed my hand. I backed away a little, my hands cold and shaky.

"How are you feeling?" My mom's brow was drawn in concern.

"A little..." I rasped, my throat dry, "...sick." I tried to take deep, slow breaths to push down the wave of nausea that threatened to overwhelm me.

Lily finally came into the room, eyeing me, her shoulders tight, a red gash crisscrossing her left cheek. She shooed the guards out into the hallway and closed the door.

"Do you need anything?" my dad asked.

"Water," I managed to say. He immediately rushed to the door and came back a couple of moments later with a plastic cup. I took the cup, which started to shake in my grasp, so my dad wrapped his fingers tightly around mine to stop me from spilling everything. After a few sips of the refreshing liquid, I leaned back onto my pillows. "What happened? Is everyone okay?" I looked at Lily, whose face was empty of all emotion.

"Yeah. Everyone's safe for now." My mom smiled.

"But what..." My head spun, black spots dancing in my vision. I squeezed my eyes shut, and an image of Sheridan's face flashed through my mind. My stomach turned upside down and I clamped my hand over my mouth, swallowing bile. I looked up at my mom, my chest tingling. "What...?"

"Shh. We don't have to talk about that right now. You need to rest. You're so pale." My mom patted my arm.

A guard burst inside, his eyes wide, his face red, his breathing hard and ragged as if he'd been running. "Elemontera is on the move," he said.

Lily chewed on her lip and ran a hand through her long black hair, grimacing. "Okay, Stefan. Keep monitoring their position. Just because they're out doesn't mean they'll find us. How many agents did they send?"

"At least twenty," Stefan said. "We can't tell how many of them are tainted elementals."

"Alert me immediately if they come our way," Lily said. Stefan nodded and slipped through the door.

I frowned. "Where are we? Where is Sheridan? I thought..." My mind was fuzzy, and I couldn't recall anything that had happened after Sheridan's arrival no matter how hard I tried. I still couldn't feel my elements either, even though I didn't have any element-blocking jewelry on me that I could see.

And if the room was element-proof itself, I'd still be able to sense my elements inside of me. Unless there was some new technology in this place that I knew nothing about. Still, that seemed unlikely, and since we were all safe, I assumed my elements were temporarily gone because I had done something to drain my elemental energy. "Did I do something with my elements?"

"You don't remember?" Lily gave me an incredulous stare.

"Remember what? I know Sheridan attacked us and then..." I bit the inside of my cheek, rubbing my stiff neck.

"I don't know. I can't recall anything after that."

"Doesn't matter, honey." My mom tucked a strand of my hair behind my ear, her smile never wavering. "You saved us all, and now we're in a safe house. You should rest for a bit and then the three of us can leave and live happily somewhere far from these monsters that want to hunt you down." She took hold of my dad's hand, and he gave her an affectionate look.

"No. No way." Lily shook her head at my mom. "You don't know how this whole thing will affect her."

"That's exactly why I want to take her away. She'll need time to recover." My mom's brow furrowed, her jaw set.

"Okay, stop." I raised my hands up, a knot forming in my throat. "Someone please tell me what happened and why you're treating me like there's something wrong with me? How can you think I'll relax if I don't even know what's going on?" Warmth filled my cheeks, followed by the feeling of a weight being lifted off me. My elements were still weak, but they were back.

"We promise we'll tell you everything, but..." my dad started to say, and my air, despite its exhausted state, reached out for his mind before I even knew what was happening. I immediately forced it back, breathing hard. My mom held out her hand toward me, but I jumped back.

"No! Don't touch me. I..." I curled my fingers into fists, pushing down my air.

"It's okay, honey," my mom said. "I suppose your

elements are acting up a bit, but it will get better."

"I can give you an element-blocking bracelet if you wish," Lily said. "Elemontera's bracelet couldn't withstand all of your energy and ended up completely destroyed. My techs might have contributed to that when they weakened it."

"Yeah, a bracelet would be great." I wasn't sure I'd have enough strength to keep my air down, so an element-blocking bracelet would help, although I didn't know how much use it would be if my elements regained some of their strength. Lily took the bracelet out of the pocket of her black leather jacket and handed it to me.

"Thanks," I said, slipping the bracelet onto my wrist. My elements calmed a little, but I had a feeling of thousands of butterflies in my stomach. Somehow I knew that my air wasn't happy, and if it weren't so weak, it would have broken through the bracelet in a second.

Pain pulsed behind my eyes and I covered my face with my hands. An image of Sheridan flashed behind my closed eyelids.

She was standing in the middle of Lily's hideout, her chin raised, her shoulders straight, a triumphant smile on her lips. "If you don't do what I say, your family and friends will die," she said, her voice slightly distorted. "Just kill him already."

The energy poured out of every pore of my body, my element rushing out. It broke through every block as if it were a knife cutting through butter. Then it found what it wanted, grasping and destroying brain signals in its way. It ended a life.

Oh, God. I cried out, my whole body shaking.

"Honey, hey!" my mom said, pulling me close to her and caressing my hair. "You're okay. I'm here now. You're safe."

"What have I done?" I whispered, tears forming in my eyes. There was only one thing I was sure of; I'd taken a life.

"You saved us," my mom said. "Sheridan and her men would have killed us all if you hadn't done what you did."

I lifted my head to look into my mom's eyes, but all I could see was the twisted smile on Sheridan's face.

My vision shifted from Sheridan to Jaiden, who was kneeling on the floor in front of me, his head bowed. He'd just told us what he'd done with his special ability; an ability that Sheridan believed I, too, had. The soldiers were pointing their weapons at my family and friends. I had to do something before Sheridan gave the order to kill everyone in the room, and I had to do it fast, but what options did I have?

The soldiers and Sheridan were protected against me, but I hadn't used all of my energy in the office, so there was a high chance I could break through the block if I really wanted. But if Sheridan just changed her mind, walked away or dropped to the ground, the soldiers would find it suspicious.

Sheridan herself had assured me of what would happen in such a situation, which meant I had to get rid of the soldiers first. But if I tried to mind-control them all at once, including Sheridan, I doubted I'd be able to break through all the blocks and successfully mind-control everyone without endangering a single person in the room.

I looked back at Jaiden, whose gaze was still glued to the floor. He was ready to die. If I just did what Sheridan asked, everyone would be safe... or not. I couldn't trust someone as crazy as Sheridan, and I couldn't kill Jaiden either. I glanced at Sheridan and her soldiers. They weren't Elemontera's soldiers. They couldn't be.

They were probably Marlau's people or hired muscle. Sheridan must have protected them against me using Elemontera's technology because she needed me to use my element, but had she had a chance to protect them against Jaiden or was she counting on the bracelet for that? I was certain Sheridan was protected against him thanks to that special implant in her spine, but what about her men? Would she have protected all of her soldiers like that too?

Maybe she'd only ensured they were safe from weaker attacks. She couldn't have known Jaiden would be with me. Or maybe she thought she knew Jaiden well enough, so she was sure he wouldn't try to fight them all. Then again, maybe she was crazy enough to believe I'd join her after she told me the truth about Jaiden, or that I'd never let him endanger my family. Or maybe she did count on the bracelet to stop him. She might have taken back the control of Elemontera's bracelets, but the bracelets had been weakened by Lily's techs. There was no way Sheridan could have known about that or fixed them so quickly.

"What are you waiting for? Kill him!" Sheridan yelled, tapping the heel of her shoe against the floor, her smile vanishing.

It was now or never. Jaiden didn't fight me as I pushed my air into his mind. I briefly closed my eyes, blocking out every sound and thought, and focused solely on one simple order: getting inside the soldiers' minds all at once and stopping them. My element pulled out from Jaiden's mind. He didn't move, but I could see a shimmering thread reaching out from him and going for the soldiers.

My air welled up inside of me and shot out, going straight for Sheridan. I had to incapacitate her before she realized what Jaiden was doing and before she decided to use some device to either stop him, order the soldiers to shoot, or alert someone else. My energy slammed into her mind, but the signals were out of my reach, my air hitting an invisible block. I shoved my element against the block harder and harder, letting all of my energy into it, every single piece of it.

The block dissolved and my air surged through Sheridan's mind. My thoughts went to Bailey and so many others she must have killed. My air grasped the signals before I could give it an order what to do, entangling them with such speed that I was dizzy. I blinked and saw Sheridan's eyes going wide, her mouth hanging open. Then she tumbled to the ground.

"Moira!" my mom's voice brought me back to reality.

I buried my face into her blonde hair, sobbing quietly. I hadn't meant to kill Sheridan. My element had done that. Or had it been all me and I didn't want to admit it to myself? My element wasn't a living thing and it couldn't have done anything without me. It had been me who thought about the deaths Sheridan had caused, and I must have somehow poured my anger into my element and mistakenly ordered it to kill instead of knock out.

"I killed Sheridan, didn't I?" I finally said, pulling back to look into my mom's eyes.

She licked her lips. "Honey..."

"So you do have the ability to kill with your mind?"

Lily said, a strange light glistening in her dark eyes.

"I guess I do," I said, sniffling.

"What about Sheridan's soldiers?" Lily asked, and I flinched, my heart skipping a beat.

"Oh, God. They're not all dead, are they?"

"They were knocked out, but they're alive," Lily said. The tension seeped out of my shoulders. Sure, those men had been ready to kill us all on Sheridan's order, but I'd have never forgiven myself if I'd forced Jaiden to kill for me.

"Did you do that too?" Lily tilted her head.

"Sort of," I said. "I ordered Jaiden to stop them. Is he okay?" I didn't know how much energy Jaiden had needed to break through the weakened bracelet and mind-control everyone at the same time.

Lily hesitated. The bracelet on my wrist started to burn and I bit my lip, clamping down my element. I really had to get back in control of my elements, because I couldn't simply mind-control people whenever they didn't immediately give me what I wanted.

"He's in custody because he confessed he was involved in deaths of innocent people," Lily finally said.

"What are you going to do with him?" I narrowed my eyes at her, my voice strained. "You can't hand him over to the cops."

"I don't have to do that. I'm authorized to deal with dangerous elementals on my own." She lifted her chin, holding her hands loosely behind her back.

My pulse sped up. "What does *that* mean? He helped us. If it hadn't been for him, we would be all dead now. If I had given in to Sheridan's request, she would have either killed you all or taken you hostage."

"You just admitted you mind-controlled him to help us. That's not the same. He's a murderer," Lily said flatly. "But the government doesn't want any info about tainted elementals out in the open, so there can't be a trial or investigation. I don't even know how we'd prove anything, but if Jaiden is considered to be too dangerous, I'll deal with him myself."

And by *deal with*, she meant kill. I struggled to get to my feet, my bracelet flying off my wrist. My mom grabbed me by the arm and pulled me back, whispering reassuring words into my ear, but I barely heard her. I was sure that Jaiden's confession would be enough for Lily to condemn him, even if she never got to hear the whole story. But as I glared at her, I realized she wouldn't be telling all of this to me if she didn't want something, especially if she knew I'd want to stop her.

Taking a deep breath, I settled back on the bed and cocked my head at her. "Mom, Dad, can you please give us a moment?" My eyes never left Lily's.

"I don't think that's a good idea," my dad said quickly.

"I won't do anything. I promise. Just want to talk to her."

"Take this." My mom pushed two element-blocking bracelets into my hand. I put them on, even though I doubted they'd work against me if I tried hard enough to break through them. Still, my parents hovered over me, glancing around uneasily.

"You don't have to worry," I said. "Lily will be fine."

"Honey, I know you would never..." my mom started to say, but my dad put his hand on her shoulder.

"Let's go," he said.

My mom sighed and got to her feet. "We'll be outside if you need us. Just yell."

"Sure." I managed a small smile. My mom gave Lily a warning look before closing the door.

Chapter 2

"What do you want?" I all but growled at Lily.

"Do you still want to go back to Elemontera like we agreed before Sheridan attacked?"

Elemontera still had to be stopped, and until I regained control of my elements, I was a danger for my parents too. They'd be safer far away from me, especially now that Sheridan was dead. Elemontera would be looking for us everywhere. "I do."

"Good." She clapped her hands, a smile breaking out on her face. "I'd appreciate it if you didn't tell your parents of what I'm about to ask of you."

"Ah, I see." I should have expected she'd want something that would piss off my parents.

"Sheridan planned to steal you away from Elemontera, so I bet she didn't tell anyone about your new ability. She couldn't have been completely sure you had it either, I guess. This means that you could solve most of our problems really quickly... if needed. Elemontera's boss is one of those problems."

"You want me to get back there and kill the boss."
My mouth went slack.

"Well, when you put it that way..." The corners of
Lily's lips went up. "I'll understand if you don't want to do
it, but your ability is unique and could be very useful. After
you release the virus and we gather all the info we need to
discredit the organization forever, the boss could still
escape, bribe someone, or find a way to continue with his
business somewhere else. But if he were to die of what
appear to be natural causes... we wouldn't have to reveal
any of the information to the public and risk the wrath of
the government."

I chewed on the insides of my mouth. Lily made the
whole thing seem so easy, but I knew it wasn't. Getting
back inside of Elemontera would be difficult, let alone
finding a way to kill the boss.

"I know taking a life isn't something you want to do
ever again, but the boss has killed hundreds, and he will
continue to destroy innocent lives until we stop him." A
somber expression flitted across Lily's face.

"You do realize I probably won't be able to bring
Elemontera to its knees on my own, even if I do get a
chance to kill the boss?"

"I do. That's why Jaiden is in custody for now. He
won't tell my interrogators or me anything no matter what
method we use, but you... he'd tell you something. Or you
could convince him to help you. One way or another."

"Okay. I'll have to talk to him and everyone. If we want to make this work, we need a very good plan," I said, ignoring the protest of my muscles as I pushed myself to my feet and leaned on the bed.

"There's something else you need to know," Lily said hesitantly. "Since Elemontera's bracelets have been destroyed, they'll need replacing. The problem is we can't really recreate the bracelets so fast, and I don't think we can fool Elemontera with our fake ones either. And we'll have to hurry with our plans. It's only a matter of time before Elemontera sends all their agents after us, and we'll have to explain Sheridan's death somehow without revealing your new ability."

"Wait, what do you mean you can't recreate the bracelets? If I go without a bracelet, Elemontera will know something strange happened and they'll make me a new one that might be even stronger." I rubbed my arms, my eyes wide. If Elemontera blocked my elements for good when I got back and left me with no options to free myself, then there would be little I could do to help anyone. I'd be trapped. "And how do you even plan to sneak in that virus? Elemontera's agents aren't stupid. They'll notice I have a fake or broken bracelet."

"We can get the virus inside with you. It won't be detectable. Trust me," Lily said with all the confidence in the world. "The bracelet is our main problem, but if you pretend Sheridan had taken it off you, then it won't be strange when you come back without one. And after they make you a new one, they can only block the amount of energy they think you have, so you'll have to be careful and never expose the full strength of your elements in places where they can monitor the levels of your elemental energy."

"Right." I stretched my stiff body, feeling a bit stronger on my feet, so I slipped into my sneakers that were next to the bed. "How long have I been out?"

"Half a day."

I ran a hand over my face. "Shit. We should hurry. Where is everyone?"

"In the living room," Lily said, going for the door. "Let me show you."

Chapter 3

As soon as I stepped through the door, I found myself in a well-lit hallway. The pale yellow walls were full of portraits and paintings. A vase with fresh flowers stood on a cabinet. Coats dangled from a hanger in front of a large mirror. As I passed by it, I briefly caught a glimpse of my pale face and the dark circles under my eyes. Lily led me into a large room with green walls. A big glass table was in the middle of it, surrounded by three large couches and two black sofas.

Everyone except Jaiden was here, including my parents. Noah was the first one to stop looking at the news on a big plasma TV and jump to his feet. He pulled me into a hug, his arms wrapping tightly around me.

"I'm so glad you're okay," he said, his blue eyes traveling my body. Marissa was the next one to hug me, while Nick and Sam waved at me, and Ashley inclined her head, her green eyes wary.

"Listen," Noah said as we made our way to the couch. "I know you planned to go back to Elemontera, but

I don't think that would be a good idea now. Lily told me her team wouldn't be able to recreate the bracelets, so if you go to Elemontera without one, you could be exposed. And even if somehow they don't discover you, I'm sure Elemontera's new bracelet will be stronger no matter what you say or show to them."

"I know that, but I hope they won't be able to block my elements completely. Maybe Sheridan didn't tell them about all of my abilities since she clearly planned to betray Elemontera all along." I didn't know if there was a device strong enough to block all of my elemental energy. It would be nice to think there wasn't, but I couldn't be sure. Still, I couldn't let doubts stop me. One look at my parents' smiling faces was enough to confirm that I had to take out Elemontera no matter what. After what happened to Bailey, I knew we'd never be safe no matter where we went.

"It was really awesome how you knocked out everyone," Nick said. "That was you, wasn't it?"

"Um, actually it was Jaiden who did that. I just... took care of Sheridan." I looked down at my hands in my lap.

"Jaiden? What do you mean, *he* did that?" Noah wrinkled his nose, his blue eyes growing cold.

"I mind-controlled him to do it," I said.

"Oh," Noah said. "Well, that definitely proves that you can't trust him, even if you succeeded in mind-controlling him once."

I raised a questioning eyebrow at him. "But I can't go to Elemontera without him."

"He's very powerful. He shouldn't be going anywhere. Not with that ability he has. If he could knock out a bunch of soldiers at the same time, just imagine what he could have done if it hadn't been you who gave the order. He might be able to kill that many people only with his mind. And even if you mind-control him to play nice, who says he won't find a loophole or fix his own brain?"

I let out a frustrated sigh. "I'm not sure I can do much without his help. He's the boss's son. He'll have access to more places than me. Even if I somehow mind-control people, I could be discovered, and a new agent like me would never get as many privileges without showing some major ability, which I can't do. I need Jaiden to come with me."

"Why don't you just use Sheridan?" Noah said, and I flinched, my mouth going slack. "She could tell you things, or you could get inside her mind and use her like a puppet."

"I... I don't understand." I swallowed past the lump forming in my throat.

"Think about it. No one in Elemontera knows about Sheridan's betrayal. We could use that," Noah said, his eyes sparkling.

I glanced at Lily, who shook her head. She clearly hadn't told Noah the truth about what had happened to Sheridan, so Noah and the others were probably thinking that Sheridan had been simply knocked out, like the soldiers. Lily must have thought it was better that not many people knew about my ability, but I didn't want to hide something so big from my friends.

"I have to tell you something," I said in a steady voice. "But it's a secret, and no one else can find out about it. If you're willing to let me mind-control you so you don't tell anyone about what I'm about to say, then you can stay and hear me out. If you don't want me in your head, then please leave now."

No one moved from their seat, expectant eyes staring at me.

"Tell us what?" Ashley asked, leaning forward.

"Sheridan is dead." My throat constricted a little as I said it.

"What? How…?" Noah's head jerked back, his voice full of disbelief.

"I killed her. With my element." I mentally braced myself for their reaction.

"That's impossible." Noah shook his head. "You're not... You..."

"Sheridan wasn't lying when she said I had the same ability as Jaiden. I know it looks like she died of a heart attack, but... I know what really happened," I said quietly.

Ashley gaped at me, her eyes full of suspicion. "How are we supposed to let you into our minds after you just said that?"

"I'm not going to hurt you. I promise." My two bracelets burned slightly, and I had a feeling my element was looking forward to reaching into someone's mind, but I knew that couldn't be true. I could control myself. All I needed was a bit more time before I dived into someone's head again.

Noah placed his warm hand over mine. "We know you won't."

"Did you know anything about this ability?" I looked into his eyes. "I mean, you kept yelling at me not to use it and..."

"I was trying to buy us some time. And I figured that if it turned out that you actually have that ability, I couldn't let you kill Jaiden because I knew how much that would have affected you. But Sheridan... it never occurred to me you could get inside her head. I thought she was protected."

"She was, but it wasn't enough."

"I have an idea," Sam said with a wide grin on his face. "Why don't we just send Moira to Elemontera so she can kill them all?"

Marissa jabbed him in the ribs with her elbow, making him groan. "Are you out of your mind?" She glared at him. "It's not that simple."

"Well, I say it is," Sam said. "People can't get inside that building with guns or blow it to pieces without getting caught, but this would be perfect. No one would know it was her."

"Yeah, I don't think she can do it that easily. And it would be impossible to explain dozens of sudden deaths in one building," Marissa said. "Then the world would find out about us and send even more organizations after us. They'd think we're all killers and..." Her eyes were wide when she looked at me, her lips slightly parted. "I didn't mean..."

"I'm not going to kill anyone," I said, my voice shaky. "We just need enough proof against them and we'll find a way to stop them from coming after us." I didn't even dream of telling anyone what Lily had suggested I do.

Noah turned to Lily. "What exactly does that virus of yours do?"

"It's designed to sneak into Elemontera's system and record everything they do, which means we'll get access to their hidden files and passwords."

My mom shifted on the couch. "And how do you plan to protect my daughter? She infects Elemontera's system with the virus, they rebuild her bracelet, and then what? You just leave her in there on her own?"

Lily licked her lips. "Unfortunately, there isn't much we can do, so yes, she'd mostly be on her own. But with her abilities, I think she can handle herself just fine until we gather enough information to get permission from the government to shut down Elemontera once and for all."

"Then simply send a random agent to infect Elemontera's system," my dad said. "Surely a trained professional can get into their headquarters somehow."

"We tried that already," Lily said. "We need someone who can access Elemontera's inner quarters—their main lab, to be exact. And we don't have any tainted elementals that we could train. It would take too much time. If we don't act fast, your daughter will be hunted down. You have to be aware of that. You can't outrun Elemontera. The safest place for her might be inside that organization. Besides, she will have a much better chance of gaining the boss's trust if she returns on her own."

"What about Sheridan?" Nick asked. "Elemontera will want to know how she died, and when they find out, they'll figure out Moira did it, and they'll never let her go."

"They won't find out. We'll blame her death on that group of elementals that attacked Elemontera the other day," Lily said. "We know they haven't been caught, so while Elemontera is busy looking for them, we'll do our little thing. That will also give Moira a chance to go out and secretly impart inside information to us."

"What about Jaiden? He knows the truth," Ashley said. "If he escapes..."

"He won't," Lily said with confidence that I didn't like. "We'll get information we need from him and make sure he doesn't reveal anything to anyone."

"Yeah, as if you can trust anything that monster says." Noah rolled his eyes.

"I have a hunch he won't lie to Moira." Lily's lips spread into a smile.

"He has his secrets. If he doesn't want to tell me something, he won't," I said.

"It doesn't matter," Lily said. "Talk to him and find a way to get some info out of him. It seems like using mind control on so many people has weakened him a lot, and he isn't regaining his strength as fast as you. I believe you could force him to tell you everything without much trouble. You just have to be ready to do it." She gave me a sharp look. "We need to find out what is the easiest way for you to get inside that lab. That's all. We can improvise the rest."

"I..." I didn't want to have to force the information out of Jaiden. Not when I suspected Lily would kill him as soon as she deemed him no longer useful. "I still think he should go with me. He's the only one like me, and I might need help when I'm back in there. I'm sure he'd help me if I needed it."

"But can you be a hundred percent sure that when it comes to choosing between you and his father, he will choose you?" Lily asked.

I averted my gaze. No, I couldn't be sure about that. Jaiden's father was a true monster, but Jaiden had stayed with him all these years despite everything his father had done, and I suspected there was still some part of him that longed for his father's approval and affection. I was just some girl who might have had more faith in him than anyone else, but I wasn't family.

"Okay, that's settled then," Lily said a moment later. "I'll discuss the best strategy with my team, and you, Moira, go talk to Jaiden before he regains his strength. I don't know for how long we can contain him in this place if his elements return to normal, so you better hurry."

"Wait! What are you going to do with him after he gives us what we need?" I asked before Lily could leave the room.

"Make sure he doesn't take another life ever again," she said calmly.

Her words cut through me like a sword, and I just sat there, my mouth hanging open. My mom and dad were at my side immediately, trying to list as many reasons as they could think of to convince me that going back to Elemontera as a double agent was the stupidest idea ever, but I blocked out their voices until all I heard was a distant buzzing in my ears.

"Hey," Noah said, placing his hand on my cheek, "he's killed innocent people. He has to pay for that."

"I..." I got to my feet, swaying a little. "I have to go talk to him."

My mom caught me by the arm. "Honey, you don't have to do this. It's better if you don't see that boy ever again. He might be only pretending he's weak. He could be waiting for you to attack and use you as his way out of here. Or he could hurt you because he knows you plan to go back to Elemontera and that his father will be in danger."

"I'll be fine." I tore away from her and hurried for the door before anyone else could stop me. Arguing voices filled the room in an instant. Everyone had a suggestion or an opinion about what I should I do, but what they all didn't seem to realize was that the decision lay with me no matter what they thought or said.

I didn't want to judge Jaiden before I talked to him. Things often weren't what they seemed, and I at least wanted to hear his side of the story. Maybe there was something he could tell me that would help me and convince Lily to spare his life. But it had to be something good, because Lily wouldn't let him live and go with me for no reason when she saw him as a threat that needed to be eliminated. In fact, she could even kill him and blame his death on Sheridan. I couldn't let that happen.

Chapter 4

I stumbled through the empty hallway until I saw one of Lily's guards, whose left arm was in a cast. He looked up at me, his hand flying to his weapon, but then the tension left his shoulders.

"I need to speak with Jaiden Maiers. Where is he?" From what I saw of the hallways and rooms, this house looked like a regular family home, not a secret base. So where on earth could they possibly be hiding Jaiden?

"Right here." The guard pressed his hand against the empty wall opposite from him, and I frowned. For a moment, nothing happened, but then something beeped and the wall parted, letting me into a dark, small cell.

Jaiden was lying on his side on the floor, his hair and forehead caked in blood. I rushed to him, placing my hand on his skin that was a bit warmer than normal. The door of the cell had already closed behind me.

"Hey, Jaiden?" I shook him a little, my heart in my throat.

He cracked his eyes open, his lips spreading into a small smile.

"Are you okay?" I asked, unable to keep the worry out of my voice.

"Yeah, just tired." He let out a loud sigh.

Mind-controlling all those soldiers must have drained him pretty badly. I helped him sit up so he could lean his back against the cold wall. He shivered a little, his eyes never leaving mine.

I licked my dry lips, unsure what to say. "Sheridan is dead," I finally said.

His eyes went wide with shock. "Did you...?"

I bobbed my head. "I didn't really mean to... I just..." I stared at the ground, settling myself next to him. "The first time you... used that ability... did you feel out of control? As if it at the same time was and wasn't you doing it?"

"What does it matter?" he said quietly. "What's done is done. You can't change it. You can tell yourself whatever you want, but it won't make you feel any better about it, and it won't change the way your friends and family look at you. People will be afraid of you, become alert whenever you're near, or they'll use you to get what they want."

I flinched, because that sounded awfully familiar. But I didn't want to dwell on it. Not now. "So what happened in the Shellbye bank?"

He took a deep breath. "Fourteen lives. I took fourteen lives that day."

"Were you on a mission?"

His shoulders stiffened. "Yeah."

"You were ordered to kill all those people?" I couldn't imagine why Elemontera would want all those people dead.

"No." He picked at his fingernails. "I was supposed to use my mind to influence our target to come out so we could take him out."

I tipped my head toward him. "So what happened?"

"I lost control, I guess. One second I was about to guide him out, and the next thing I knew he convulsed and the whole place exploded." He gazed at the wall far away, his shoulders sagging.

"And after that?"

"My father figured out I had the ability to kill without leaving any trace of my element anywhere, so he sent me on specific missions, some for Elemontera, some for the government."

I could barely breathe. That meant most of Jaiden's missions were kill missions. I couldn't imagine what I'd do if Elemontera found out about my ability and forced me to be their assassin. "How many people did you have to...?"

"Seven."

"Were they innocent people?" I didn't even know why I was asking that.

"Not really, but that doesn't change the fact that I killed them." His dark eyes met mine. "So what information did they send you to get out of me? I imagine you don't want to go back to Elemontera after what happened."

I hesitated.

"It's okay. I know they wouldn't let you in here just to find out a story they don't have interest in hearing. I bet they've already decided what they're going to do with me." He traced lines over the dusty ground with his fingers.

"The plan hasn't changed. I'm going back to Elemontera," I said, and he looked up at me with wide eyes.

"You can't go there. You'll get yourself killed!"

"That's why I need your help." I covered his hand with mine, and he eyed me suspiciously. "I want you to come with me."

"You want me to go back to Elemontera with you to save you when you fail," he said flatly.

He said *when*, not *if*, which meant that he didn't believe anyone could do anything against Elemontera. I ignored his comment and nodded.

"I don't think Lily will let me go even if I agreed to help you."

"She will," I said confidently.

"Okay." He perked up a bit, his eyes boring into mine. "But whatever happens, you can't let my father know about your ability, and you mustn't use it anywhere near devices that can measure levels of elemental energy. I don't even know if they can somehow recognize that you could have that ability just by looking at the levels, but it's better not to risk it."

"I won't tell him. I'm not crazy. But what about the bracelets? Can they detect something like that?"

"No. They can block your elemental energy, but they can't really read it."

"Okay, that's good. Lily says we'll blame Sheridan's death on those rogue elementals so your father doesn't suspect me and has his attention elsewhere." I twirled a strand of my hair around my finger.

Jaiden's whole body went rigid, his face paling. "You can't do that!"

"Why not?" My eyebrows shot upward. "It's not like Elemontera isn't already searching for them. And those elementals did try to kill us all, so..."

"No, if Elemontera finds out there are more elementals who can do what I can, they'll try to force every elemental to develop this ability. It's better if they think it's a unique ability." He wiped the beads of sweat off his forehead with the sleeve of his shirt.

I watched him for a moment and wondered if he was worried his father would easily find a replacement for him in Elemontera. But maybe he was right; if Elemontera thought I could somehow do the same as he could, wouldn't they try everything to get me to use that ability? That would be a huge problem for all of us.

"Then we should destroy the body. If he can't find her, he'll never know what happened to her," I said.

"He'll go to the end of the world to find out, and that could put many people in danger. You don't know him like I do. Even if Lily's team fakes an explosion and plants bodies inside, he'll still discover the truth and he'll be more suspicious than ever." Jaiden ran a shaky hand through his hair, wincing, his fingers coming away with blood.

"But it would give us some time to..." I had no idea how else to explain Sheridan's death. Any elemental energy could be detected and traced back to the person who used it, so it would be hard to blame someone else. Destroying the body seemed like the best option.

"No," he said determinedly. "If I go back with you, I'll tell him I killed her."

"What?" I gaped at him. "You can't! He'll..."

"He'll be pissed off, yeah." He pulled his knees up to his chest, as if bracing himself for his father's wrath. "But he won't kill me. Not if we explain everything to him."

I wanted to ask him how sure he was of that, but I bit down on my lip. "You said Sheridan was your father's lover. Will he believe she betrayed him?"

"He'll have to." Jaiden chewed on his lip.

"How long has she been in Elemontera, anyway? She said that she had gone to Elemontera because she couldn't find me, but that would mean Marlau knew about me for longer than we all thought."

He was pensive for a moment, his brow furrowed. "At least four years. You can't get into Elemontera's inner circle in a few weeks. She and Marlau must have been waiting until you were old enough, or they had something else in mind."

"But that doesn't make sense. They couldn't have known I'd have another element. And Marlau thought I was a carrier..." I rubbed my forehead in confusion. "So they couldn't have been looking for me because of my abilities. I guess they just wanted me to take over the company or whatever. But I believe you said that before tainted elementals appeared, Elemontera was different. Were they looking for people or what? I mean, I want to understand why Sheridan went to Elemontera for help."

Most elementals developed their elements in adolescence, so some four years ago, maybe a couple of tainted elementals appeared for the first time, but Elemontera couldn't have found out about them immediately. My second element had come out pretty late, but that didn't mean it was the same for everyone else.

Jaiden looked away. "They were looking for people. For experiments. So yeah, she'd be able to find you sooner."

"But I wasn't hiding anywhere. Anyone could have found me... unless they didn't know my identity. If Marlau somehow found out he had a granddaughter, but he didn't know my name or anything else about me, would Elemontera have helped?"

Jaiden nodded. "It would be his best bet aside from going to the cops. Elemontera used various things to find elementals and magic disease carriers, and they were one of the first to have a device to detect various properties of elements. They might have tried looking for you based on your element, but they couldn't have gotten a reading until…"

"Until I developed fire, which was my father's element. Of course they'd assume I inherited his element and not my mother's." I rolled my eyes. "I still want to know what Sheridan's connection was to Marlau. I mean, everything they told me could be a lie, so…"

"Don't worry about that now."

"Right." I blinked. "I still think we should just hide the body and buy us some time. Then your father won't be able to blame anyone."

"You don't want to find out how he is when he's obsessed and paranoid about something, trust me." He grimaced.

I wasn't sure if I could trust him. All of this seemed like his attempt to convince me that taking him with me would be the best option. I couldn't really blame him for trying to do everything to save his own life, and I definitely didn't want him to die, so if he was willing to do this, so was I. And if he took the blame for Sheridan's death, even Lily wouldn't have that to complain about.

"So do you know how to get inside the main lab?" I asked.

He wrinkled his brow, eyeing me with mistrust. "Lily wants you to get the data from researches and experiments, doesn't she? That would be her evidence against Elemontera."

I kept my face expressionless. "Maybe."

"We can find a way to get you inside, but I won't say anything until we're both back in Elemontera."

"Okay, so we have a deal. You'll come with me, and if you betray me, your father will hear the truth about your involvement in the whole thing and about my new ability." A slow smile spread across my lips, but I knew it didn't reach my eyes.

"If you don't trust me, you can mind-control me right now," he said.

I shook my head. "My elements..."

He moved toward me and pulled me into his arms so my head rested on his shoulder, his warmth enveloping me. "Your elements will be fine. Don't let the doubt or fear stop you. Your elements are tied to your emotions. If you feel like you can't do something, they're more likely to fail or act out."

I groaned. "I know. I just..."

"I'd say give yourself time, but we don't have it. I don't know where Lily's men brought us, but if we're still in the city, Elemontera could find us soon."

"Right." I reluctantly extracted myself from his arms and forced myself to my feet. "I'll talk to Lily and the others, and see what they say."

"You do that." He gave me an encouraging nod.

Without another look at him, I strode to the door and banged on it. I could feel the guard's intense gaze on me as he let me out. And just like that, I knew he was one of those rare few Lily trusted and had told about my special ability.

"Make sure there's one guard inside the cell at all times. If you don't…" my voice trailed off and the guard swallowed hard, nodding. Now that Jaiden was awake, I couldn't leave him alone in that claustrophobic cell.

"Thanks," I said, and strode down the hallway. Lily might not be pleased to hear that I had to take Jaiden with me, but she'd have to trust me, just like I trusted her with the safety of my parents while I was gone.

Chapter 5

After who knew how many hours of trying to come up with a decent plan that would be to everyone's satisfaction, we still hadn't reached an agreement.

"I still think you shouldn't go back, let alone with him. Your mind control might not even work on him," Noah said, scratching his chin. "And who says he can't heal his own mind like you did with Nick's and erase all your mind control?"

I didn't even know if healing one's own brain was possible. "I don't think he knows how to do that, and if he tried, he could mess up his brain like he did with that guy whose mind he tried to fix. Besides, it wouldn't be worth the risk for him."

"You don't know how his mind works. He's been lying to us, hiding things, putting us all in danger, and he has the ability to kill us all, so I'm sorry if you think I'm overreacting. And you'd also have to mind-control him not to tell about any of this or where we're going, because if he exposes our location or the location of the hideout on

Roivenna..." Noah paced up and down the room. "And there are so many things he could tell or show to his father that could jeopardize the whole mission and endanger your family's lives too. I doubt you can remember or think of every possible loophole when you mind-control him."

I sat on the sofa, running a hand over my face. The others were just quietly observing us, which only made me more unnerved.

"And don't forget he murdered innocent people. Actually, never forget that," Noah said.

"He's not a cold-blooded killer! His father sent him on kill missions, and what happened in Shellbye was an accident. He didn't mean to do it!" I realized I'd raised my voice too much.

Lily just watched, her lips pressed into a tight line. "I understand that you care about him and that you think that the two of you are similar, but forget about how you feel about him for a second, and use your brain. We can still go with our initial plan. Jaiden is weak right now. Mind-control him to tell you how to get into the main lab. I'm sure he knows something. Maybe even a secret entrance. Think about it. You wouldn't have to work for Elemontera anymore. If he really cared about you, he'd already tell you, and the fact that he doesn't want you to tell his father about your ability only confirms what I said before. He'll choose his father over you anytime."

Noah gave me a hard look. "Lily's right, and Jaiden's killed other people, you know. Not only those with his mind. Remember that guy who came after you in the city and Jaiden shot him in the head? We don't know how many people he really killed. He could be lying about everything."

I felt my bracelets burning on my skin, my elements lost in the whirl of emotions surging through me. "He's not as weak as you think. He wouldn't let me mind-control him, and if he thought I was trying to trick him, he could even lash out and hurt someone. Is that what you want? To ruin our only chance of getting inside that lab? What if there's no other way? What if he's the only one who can walk me inside? How many people do you know who can do that? Or you think I can just mind-control or kill my way inside?"

Lily closed her eyes, leaning her head on the wall. My element shot through the bracelets, the burning sensation going away, and surged toward Lily. Noah gasped, and Marissa, who was the closest to me, grabbed my arm. I looked at her and my element slammed back into me.

Lily cocked her head. "Um, what just happened?" Her eyes narrowed at me. "Did you just...?"

I clenched my fingers into fists. "Sorry, I lost control of myself for a moment." One part of me wondered if there was a way to make sure none of the elementals like me could see the shimmering thread. When Jaiden had been mind-controlling Kenna in that alley in the city, I couldn't do anything to help her because I couldn't see the damn shimmering. Maybe it all depended on how much energy was used to create the shimmering and not on how strong the observer was. Huh. I was getting tired of all of this. "Let's end this discussion once and for all. Jaiden is coming with me or I'm not going back."

Lily rolled her eyes, and Noah stared at me in disbelief. I was glad my parents weren't around to express their disagreement.

"I hope you realize you could be putting everyone at risk," Lily said.

"Let me deal with Jaiden. I'll make sure nothing goes wrong." I hoped I wasn't making a big mistake.

"Fine," Lily said through gritted teeth. "If I must agree to this, I'd rather agree knowingly than have you force me to change my mind." She pushed herself off the wall and strolled out of the room. Well, that had been easier than I'd expected.

"Moira..." Noah knelt in front of me, placing his hands on my knees, his blue eyes searching mine. "I know you think you have to do this and that taking Jaiden with you is the only way, but you're still shaken after what happened. Even your elements aren't in control. You should think about this when your head is clearer. We don't have much time, but Elemontera still didn't find us, so you can still..."

"I won't change my mind. I'm just..." I fidgeted, aware that my element wanted out. And I wouldn't really get an opportunity to use it here, but in Elemontera... there would be plenty of opportunity.

"Please, just think about it. Your new ability is dangerous and you might need time to be able to control it. You'll be safer far away from Elemontera. Come with us... Come with me." His eyes sparkled with fervor. "You can heal Kenna's brain and we can all leave the island together, and find a new hideout. We can gather our strength, find support, and then we can face anyone we want and take Elemontera down. We can even go on that date we never went on."

I got to my feet, putting some distance between us. "No." My arm briefly flickered with fire, and I had to take a deep breath to push it back. "I need a day or two, and my elements will be perfectly fine. This is our best chance to take Elemontera down. If we wait until we get stronger, they'll get stronger too. And they'll go after my parents, my relatives... I can't let that happen and just sit in some dark place until we figure out what to do."

"Looks like you made up your mind." Noah gave me a bitter smile.

"You're going to help me," I said. "Elemontera will send me on a mission, probably very soon, because they'll need more agents to capture those elementals. If I have something to tell you, I'll look at one of the city surveillance cameras. I'm sure Lily and her team will be trying to monitor my every move outside Elemontera.

You'll just have to find me and meet me somewhere when other agents are away."

"Can't someone else do that? I'd rather look after the others than be your personal messenger." He clenched his jaw.

"You can do both. I assume you're strong enough now to fly from the city to Roivenna and back. And if you somehow get captured, you'll have better chances of escape than any of the others." He had experience in dodging Elemontera's agents, and I knew he wouldn't let himself get caught.

"Okay, fine." He clasped his hands tightly, his knuckles white. "But I still think you could find your way into the lab without Jaiden. He's only trying to save his skin, so he'd promise you now whatever he thought you wanted to hear."

I shrugged. "I guess we'll see." With a cold smile on my face, I walked out of the room.

Chapter 6

My insides wanted to flip inside out as Elemontera's headquarters came into view. It had taken me four days to regain my full strength and mind-control everyone so they didn't reveal any info that could put us all in danger. But now that Jaiden and I were supposed to walk back inside that damn building as if nothing had happened, my heart thudded loudly in my chest, my throat constricting.

Jaiden slipped his fingers into mine. "Nothing bad will happen to you. I promise."

I straightened my shoulders, giving his hand a little squeeze, then let go. Lily had sent one of her men to tip Elemontera off about the location of Sheridan's body. It had been Lily's idea to distract Elemontera and get their best agents out of the building. If we were lucky, maybe the boss wouldn't be in the headquarters, so I could find the lab before he came back, and infect the main computer in the lab, but that sounded too much like wishful thinking.

My arm still stung like hell around the spot where Lily's team had pierced my skin so they could slip a tiny chip-like device underneath. Apparently, that was the only way I could sneak in with the device without triggering any alarms. The problem was that I'd have to open the wound again to push the device out when I needed to use it. The sole thought of digging through a fresh wound made me nauseous.

As soon as we stepped through the door, the guards pointed their guns at us, their eyes wide. Jaiden raised his hands, a smile spreading over his lips. "Really? We go through all the trouble to come back here and this is our welcome?"

The guards looked at each other, checking something on the computer behind the desk next to them. They must have used facial recognition to see we were just agents, although I was sure they knew Jaiden very well. They had to have seen Elemontera's best agent before.

"Where are your bracelets, agents?" one of the guards narrowed his hazel eyes at us.

"Didn't anyone tell you? We were captured. The enemy took the bracelets." Jaiden waved his hands, inviting them to take a better look at us. We'd made sure to rip our clothes and have some cuts and bruises so everyone would believe we'd indeed run away from our captors. I was glad about that, because at least then no one would ask why I had a gash in my left arm.

The guard sighed after one of the devices behind his desk beeped, making me jump. "Okay, go on. And make sure you report to your superiors."

We immediately started for the elevator, hoping we wouldn't run into many people. I gritted my teeth to stop myself from reacting as the eyes of familiar cameras stared at me once again. God, I hated this place so much, and now I had come back to destroy it. But when we reached our floor, I noticed glowing yellow devices at each side of the elevator door. "What's that?"

Jaiden swore under his breath. "Elemental detectors. They constantly monitor the levels of elemental energy. The alarm goes off if you use your element around them."

So Elemontera had upgraded their security. Wonderful. But not entirely surprising. The rogue elementals had torn through Elemontera's agents, and I was sure the boss and the others wondered what would happen if those elementals found their way into the building. Luckily for us, the hallway was empty, and it seemed like Lily's plan had worked. Most of the agents had to be outside, so only a couple remained, but the guards were still here, which meant we couldn't exactly do whatever we wanted.

"Follow me," Jaiden said, going straight for the hallway that led to another elevator. We got inside without any trouble, and he pressed a button for the floor I'd never been to, because I wasn't allowed to go there, but nothing happened.

"Shit." Jaiden slammed his hand against the buttons. "We don't have the bracelets. Of course we can't go to any floor other than the main one. Wait here."

He hurried outside and waved at a guard who was just coming around the corner. "Hey, a little help here. We need to get new bracelets from the lab, so can you just press the button in the elevator? We can't do it ourselves."

The guard hesitated, but he must have recognized Jaiden, so he strolled toward us and pressed the button.

"Thanks." Jaiden gave him a wide grin.

My heart thudded in my chest as we found ourselves in a long hallway with red walls and thick black carpet that covered the floor completely. Aside from two or three doors, it looked empty. What the hell? The main lab was somewhere here? The cameras were everywhere, along with multiple glowing yellow devices. Would even a little bit of elemental energy trigger an alarm? I didn't want to find out.

Jaiden stopped in front of an empty wall, pressing on it with both hands. Before I could ask him what the hell he was doing, a triangular piece of the wall pulled itself in, revealing a keypad. Jaiden punched in four numbers, and I did my best to remember them in case I had to come back here alone. The whole wall parted and let us into a new metallic-looking hallway. For some reason, I had a feeling that whoever had built Lily's hideout house had participated in creating this mechanism too. The whole 'secret passage in a wall' thing seemed so similar.

We followed the hallway that was full of various yellow devices and alarms until we reached the end. A huge glass door stood in front of us, showing another hallway with numerous doors, and people in white coats hurrying around. Six guards were in front of the door, and that was when I realized this was the place I was looking for; this was the entrance into the lab. The main computer had to be somewhere behind that door.

"We need new bracelets. Ours are gone," Jaiden said to the guards, his voice light and friendly.

"You can't go inside," a tall guard said, running a hand through his short black hair. "Boss's orders."

"So we're supposed to walk around without bracelets? Come on, we can't even get to our rooms." Jaiden crossed his arms, annoyance creeping into his voice. "And if we can't get anywhere, then we can't do our jobs. Somehow I don't think the boss will be pleased when he hears that."

The guard trudged closer, a smirk on his face. "Well, looks to me like you got here just fine, and as far as I remember, you're not allowed to set foot anywhere near this lab, *Jaiden*." He spit out his name like a curse.

I considered using my element to mind-control the guards, but the energy detectors were all over the place. One wrong move and the whole building would be alerted, and then we'd never get to do what we had to and escape in time.

"Then at least let her go in. She won't break anything," Jaiden said, curling his lip.

"No." A vein pulsed in the guard's neck as he glared at Jaiden.

"If the boss were here..." Jaiden started to say.

"Oh, he *is* here, all right," a voice behind our back said, and we turned around, finding ourselves face to face with the boss. His black suit was slightly wrinkled, his dark hair disheveled as if he'd been in a great hurry. His cold gray eyes were pinned on Jaiden. "My office. Now. Both of you." His gaze raked over me as he turned and started down the hallway.

"But the bracelet..." I started to say, and Jaiden caught my arm, shaking his head. I closed my mouth. The boss wasn't supposed to be here, but now that he was, we had no other choice but to follow him. I glanced once at the glass door, hoping I'd get back here sooner rather than later. Lily had been so sure the boss would go see Sheridan's body himself, based on what Jaiden had told me about his father's affection for her, but now I didn't know what to think.

I was lightheaded as we stepped through the door of the boss's office, and I realized this room had the same element-blocking walls as his private office. Even the desk looked the same as the one on which Jaiden had been kissing me when we were looking for that device.

Making sure my elements were safely tucked inside of me, I wiped all expression off my face. The boss seated himself in his big leather chair, his face grim. We stood there in front of him, unsure what to do. The boss opened one of the drawers, but I couldn't see what he was doing.

"So you two came back..." he said coldly. "We've been looking for you all over the city. Where have you been?"

"Anton Marlau's men kidnapped us," I said. "They were after me."

The boss regarded me for a moment. "I believe that man is dead. Did his ghost order your kidnapping? And how come you couldn't have fought off a few regular elementals? I assume he couldn't have found an army of tainted elementals."

"It was Sheridan, sir," Jaiden said. "She was a spy. A traitor. She took control of our bracelets, and then it was easy for Marlau's men to overpower us and take us to an abandoned building. Sheridan wanted Moira to take over her grandfather's company or something. She was loyal to Marlau, not to us."

The lines around the boss's mouth tightened as he glared at Jaiden. "Were some of those tainted elementals that we've been hunting there too?"

"No, sir" Jaiden said. "We..."

The boss stood up so suddenly that I took a step back. His face was a mask of fury. "You couldn't have known if she'd been mind-controlled, could you?"

Jaiden licked his lips, lowering his gaze.

"She wasn't," I said. "She knew things about my grandfather that no one could have known if they hadn't been close. A bunch of teenagers couldn't have found that out. And she had this strange symbol with lions' heads on her uniform just like the guards." I hoped mentioning the symbol would revive the boss's memory. He had to have seen the tattoo on Sheridan's back. There'd be no doubt about her betrayal.

An emotion flickered through the boss's eyes, but it was gone in a second. His jaw was tight, his teeth clenched. "All right, let's assume you're right. What happened? How did you escape?"

"She wanted to take me away. I'm not sure exactly where," I said. "She disabled my bracelet completely and took it off after I agreed to do what she wanted. I mean, I was pretending... I..."

"What about our other agents?" the boss asked. "Nick Elinders and Noah Boine?"

"They weren't with us when we were taken," Jaiden said. "We haven't seen them. When Sheridan took off Moira's bracelet, we used the opportunity, and Moira freed me, so we fought our way out of there."

"Ah, you fought, of course." The boss let out a laugh, then his face darkened, his right arm tensing. "And yet, those men you mention weren't there when our team arrived. Only she was... dead. Heart attack, they say."

"What? But they were knocked out or dead. It's impossible..." I feigned surprise. We couldn't have handed the men we had captured to Elemontera because they'd have ended up dead. Lily would make sure the men ended up in jail, and I'd already manipulated their minds so they wouldn't remember a thing.

"You should have stayed where you were! Waited for us! Captured them all!" The boss was yelling, his face red, but he didn't move; his whole body was rigid like a statue. "Instead you decided to fly all the way across the city to come here for no good reason and ruin everything!"

"Sir, we didn't know how many men Sheridan and Marlau had hired. If we had stayed, we could have been recaptured. It took a lot of energy to..."

"To kill her. To take her from me!" He raised his arm, and I gasped as he pointed a gun at Jaiden's head. "Give me one reason why I shouldn't just end your life right here right now. Sheridan might have been involved with strange things, but you should have let *me* deal with it. Instead you killed her and you let the others escape! Who knows what they'll do now!"

My whole body was shaking, my elements wanting out even through the block of the room. I dug my nails into my skin, ready to rush the boss if needed. Jaiden was barely breathing, standing perfectly still.

"You need me," he said, his voice so full of certainty that I wanted to punch his father in the face, hug Jaiden to myself, and tell him that this was all wrong. That his ability shouldn't be the only thing keeping him alive here. But his father wrinkled his nose, and lowered the gun. I let out the breath I hadn't even known I'd been holding.

"You're right. I do need you, but I don't want you here right now." He pressed a button on what looked like a phone, and the door swung open. Two guards walked inside. "Take him away," the boss said calmly. "Room One."

Jaiden flinched, his jaw tight, but he didn't say anything or try to fight the guards as they grabbed him by the arms and dragged him out. I had no idea what or where that room was, and dread filled my stomach.

"He said you had freed him. Why?" The boss ran a hand over his desk, his eyes locking with mine.

"I didn't want to make a wrong choice that would put my parents' lives at risk." I lowered my eyes, hoping he'd believe I was just a scared little girl who wouldn't dare disobey Elemontera's orders.

"Well, you made the right choice. Thanks to you, your parents will keep on breathing," he said. "We have eyes on them every second of the day."

I wondered what he'd think if it were discovered that Lily had been fooling them and feeding them false information about my parents. "Am I dismissed?"

"Yes," the boss said. "You'll be escorted to your room and you'll stay there until we make you a new bracelet. Surely you could use some rest."

I inclined my head and hurried to the door before he could change his mind and ask more questions. I wasn't looking forward to being stuck in my damn room again and getting a new bracelet, but I knew that the idea of completing my secret mission on my first day back was too good to be true. I'd have to be patient and find the right opportunity. At least now I knew where the lab was.

"Moira," the boss said just as I was about to pass through the door, and I slowly turned around. "I see potential in you. If it weren't for my idiot son, I'm sure you would have done better." He watched my face carefully. "I see you're not surprised, so I take it you know he's my son, as I expected. It would be wise if you kept your mouth shut about all of this, especially about Sheridan. You're not irreplaceable here. Do you understand?"

"Yes." My head throbbed because my element was begging me to release it and just crush the boss's brain, but whatever that was protecting the room was pretty good, because all I could do was make myself dizzy.

"Good. Now go."

I didn't have to be told twice. A guard waited for me outside, and I had to breathe deeply and shove my elements down, or I'd have triggered all the alarms on the way to my room.

Chapter 7

I turned off the alarm clock on my nightstand before it could pierce the air with its annoying sound. It was my second day in Elemontera. How wonderful. It seemed as if I'd never been out at all. Sitting up in the bed, I stared at the metallic-looking wall. I had to find a way to get into the lab, and I really, really needed to get myself on some kind of a mission because I had a feeling I could burst from all the energy stored inside of me.

I pressed my hand to my forehead, my skin unusually warm. My fire must have been trying to get closer to the surface. And I really had to stop myself from thinking about Jaiden, because the whole thing had been his idea and he must have known what he was doing. But I wished I at least knew whether he was okay.

His father might not want to kill him, but that didn't mean Jaiden wouldn't get hurt. Pushing the thought away, I jumped to my feet. Maybe a cold shower would clear my mind and calm my elements. It was a good thing one of

Elemontera's techs tweaked the door so I could get out of my room without a bracelet.

"Moira Arnolds," a guard said as I emerged from the bathroom, "come with me."

I followed him down the hallway, wondering where we were going. My heart sank when I realized the guard was taking me straight to the boss's office.

"There you go," the boss said, his face cheerful. He'd forgotten his grief over Sheridan rather quickly, or maybe he'd finally gotten it through his thick skull that she'd tricked him and betrayed him. That must have been a huge hit for his ego. Getting up from his chair, he twirled something shiny in his fingers. "Please sit."

I settled myself in one of the soft chairs and carefully watched him as he rounded the desk and stopped in front of me.

"Your arm," he said, reaching out for me, and I realized that the shiny thing he was holding was a bracelet. I reluctantly lifted my arm, trying not to cringe when his fingers wrapped around my wrist. He was humming something to himself as he secured the bracelet in its place. I pulled my hand back as soon as he let go, and he smiled at me, grabbing a device off the desk. He carefully positioned the device against the bracelet. A soft red light started to pulse on the device.

"Your energy levels seem a bit higher than before. That's quite interesting," he said. "The bracelet was tweaked a bit so it could handle all of your energy, but I hope we won't have to block your elements anytime soon."

I swallowed past the lump in my throat. What if there was a way for them to see that I now had the same ability as Jaiden? Or had that ability already existed before, without my knowledge? I couldn't be sure, but I hoped the bracelet couldn't block all of my elemental energy completely.

"There. All done." He tossed the device on the desk and returned to his seat. "Do you think you're ready for work?"

"Of course," I said, fighting the urge to rub my wrist.

"There's something from Sheridan's office I want you to retrieve for me before the investigators come." He eyed me, as if trying to decide if I was up to the job.

"Um, okay. What should I look for?"

"Do you remember that device Jaiden and you acquired during your..." He frowned. "What was it? First or second mission? Well, doesn't matter anyway. The device should have been delivered to a certain person a long time ago, but Sheridan failed to complete the task. I want you to get that device and take it to a lab."

My pulse sped up. Was he talking about the lab I needed to get to? But that would be ridiculous. Why would he need an agent for that? If he just wanted the device transferred, almost anyone could have carried it from one floor to the other. "I can do that."

"Good. Do you have your tablet?" He raised an eyebrow at me, and I nodded. "I'll send you the directions. You'll find Victor Rice and you'll give the device to him and only to him. No one else can touch that thing. Do you understand?"

"Yes." Of course it was another lab, but maybe I'd get the opportunity to get into Elemontera's too. The boss obviously trusted me, or at least he was taking a risk with me, which made me wonder where Jaiden was.

"The device should be treated with care," he added.

"Of course. Biochemical weapons are as dangerous as they are fascinating." I managed a small smile.

The boss's eyebrows went up. "Don't make me regret my decision. You're a field agent, not a scientist."

I bit down on my lip. Okay, my attempt to try to convince him I could join his scientists and work with them had failed. "Is there anything else I need to do?"

"No, just that. You may go now, and be quick about it."

I just gave him a curt nod, got to my feet and rushed outside. A smile quirked the corners of my lips. I'd just gotten an excuse to go through Sheridan's stuff. Maybe I'd find something useful. My only fear was that someone would be supervising me, but when I got to the door of Sheridan's office, no one was waiting for me.

The door opened as soon as I stepped closer, and I went inside before anyone could see me. Closing the door,

I looked around the small office. The camera was in the corner to my left, so I turned my back to it and went over to the empty desk. I couldn't exactly look for the device in the drawers because I suspected it was too big, although I'd never really seen it out of the bag.

Turning to the closet, I opened it and found numerous black bags. The device had to be somewhere in here, but a bag with Sheridan's lion symbol caught my eye. Carefully hiding myself from the camera, I opened the bag and realized it was full of papers. I quickly flipped through them, but didn't see anything remotely interesting.

Actually, the content of almost all of the bags was completely useless. Sheridan hadn't been stupid enough to leave evidence about her involvement with Marlau somewhere where anyone could find it. I grabbed the bag that was hidden at the back of the closet and pulled it out. Unzipping it, I saw the edge of the device inside. Gently grasping the round surface of the device, I took it out of the bag.

It was mostly black and its middle part looked like an hourglass, with two round globes that were filled with some sort of liquid. I immediately tucked the device safely back into the bag. Who knew what that thing contained? The last thing I needed was to break it and get myself killed. Although, infecting the whole of Elemontera with a deadly virus didn't sound like a terrible idea, but they'd probably stop the spread of the virus before it reached anyone important.

I was about to shut the closet door when a small paper caught my eye. I picked it up and realized it was an address. Making sure the cameras couldn't see a thing, I slipped the paper into my pocket. Maybe it was Sheridan's address. I didn't know if she'd lived in Elemontera or somewhere else.

When I grabbed my tablet, the map was already flashing on the screen, and I needed a moment to figure out the building I needed to go to was only a couple of blocks away. As I walked down the hallway, I wondered if I should simply contact Noah and hand the device over, then claim I'd been attacked. But failing this mission wasn't an option.

The boss would never trust me after that, and I'd never get to the floor where the lab was, let alone get into the lab itself. I hoped I wasn't making the wrong decision, because if this weapon got into the hands of a psycho, it could probably destroy thousands of lives. Or maybe not.

As I walked down the busy streets, I loosened the iron control I had over my elements, letting my fire warm the air around me. All too soon, I found myself in front of what looked like a store. Double-checking the address, I pushed the red-and-white door and peeked inside. It actually was a real store, its space filled with dozens of shelves with groceries and various products.

I stopped dead in my tracks. Surely this couldn't be it. But as I was about to turn around and walk away, I noticed a metal door at the back of the store that didn't quite fit with the white and red tones the whole store seemed to favor. Glancing over my shoulder, I padded around the shelves and stepped in front of the door, which cracked open all on its own.

I followed the dark hallway until I reached a white room. A tall, thin man with short silver hair was leaning over a table that was full of various glasses and containers filled with strange liquids. To my right, there was another door, but it was closed.

"Um, hello?" I said, and the man jumped, nearly knocking over one of the containers.

"For the love of God of Magic!" he yelped, facing me, his blue eyes wary. "Who are you?"

"I'm looking for Victor Rice."

The man ran his hands over his long white coat. "You found him. How can I help you?"

"I came to deliver this to you. From Elemontera," I said cheerfully, placing the bag on an empty stool.

"Oh." The old man didn't seem too surprised, and he slowly opened the bag. As he took a quick look at the contents, the wrinkles on his forehead became more prominent.

"Everything okay?" I asked.

"Yes. You may go, girl." He waved his hand at me, as if shooing me away.

Too bad he wasn't one of those chatty people. Knowing a little more about what was in the damn device would be helpful. But I had no choice other than to leave since I was unwilling to risk using mind control on him. If Lily and the others had already seen where I was on nearby cameras, I hoped they wouldn't break into this place too soon. We need to get that device, but not before Elemontera was gone and no one could blame me for leading Lily and her team straight to one of Elemontera's secret labs.

I really hoped the old guy wouldn't use the device or do something with it in the near future, because that would be really unfortunate—although there were probably plenty of even more dangerous devices out in the world that we didn't know about. This one couldn't be so important if the boss had let me walk out with it as if I were delivering flowers. Unless he'd sent me because he knew no one would ever suspect I had something valuable with me. Damn it. The more I thought about it, the more my head hurt. At least I wouldn't be disappointing the boss this time.

Chapter 8

I paced up and down one of Elemontera's long hallways, gnawing on my fingernails. My elements wanted to be used, and I'd spent a week already inside of this damn building. No matter how hard I strained my ears around people, I hadn't heard a single whisper about Jaiden or where he could be. As I passed the lunchroom, a familiar face caught my eye. One of the guards who'd escorted Jaiden out of the office on the day we'd come back to Elemontera was sitting alone at one of the tables eating some kind of a soup.

I headed toward him, grabbing a plate and some bread off the counter. Making sure no one was observing me too closely, I sat across from the guard, who lifted his eyes toward me and gave me a slightly surprised look.

"Hey," I said with a smile. Luckily for me, there were no elemental energy detectors in here, so I let my air slip out under the table and go toward the guy, just so other elementals like me couldn't see the shimmering thread.

"Cheer up, dude," I said, tilting my head. "What's your name?"

"Tommy," he said, and his lips pulled into a slow smile. Better. Now whoever saw us wouldn't assume that I was harassing the guy or forcing him to talk to me.

My element dove in between his brain signals, enjoying the rush of power. "Do you know where Jaiden is?" I said as quietly as possible.

"Yes, he's in Room One."

I took a spoonful of my soup, not breaking eye contact with the guard. He'd stopped eating. "Act normal, please." My hair was hiding my face enough that the cameras couldn't read my lips. I wondered if they'd find it suspicious that I was talking to a guard, but I hoped they either wouldn't pay attention or that they'd come after I found out what I needed. "Where is that room?"

A frown creased his brow, but I grasped his mind. "Room One," I said. "Can you take me there?"

"No. You don't have permission to go there. Only Joe and I do."

"And why is that? Wouldn't you take someone else there if there was a good reason?" I needed to find a way to get to Jaiden, or at least figure out what the hell was going on.

"No. Only the boss can give you permission."

Which wouldn't happen in a million years, so I wouldn't even bother to try. Glancing to my left, I noticed one of the men at the door was watching us, and I knew I had to hurry. "Is that room on a restricted floor? Or can anyone access it, but not the room itself?"

"Not many can go there, but yes, more people can get permission to access that floor."

"And why do other people go to that floor?" I asked in my sweetest voice.

"To get new devices or replacements."

"What kind of devices?" I raised an eyebrow at him.

"Alarm clocks, magic level readers, tablets..."

"Tablets?" The corners of my lips quirked up. "So if my tablet was broken and I needed a new one, and I came to you... Would you take me to that floor?"

"Yes, if it's urgent."

My air flashed through his mind, and I had to pull it back a little to stop it from smashing something. The guard's eyes were glassy, his face expressionless.

"How many cameras are there in and around Room One? What about the detectors of elemental energy?" I held up my hand, pretending to scratch my cheek while covering my mouth from prying eyes.

"None."

"What?" I gaped at him. Elemontera had security in every damn corner of this place, so why weren't there any in that room?

"Are you sure? You didn't by any chance forget about them?" If Jaiden had been tasked with mind-controlling the guards, then maybe the guard wouldn't remember the cameras even if they were there. But memories couldn't be completely erased.

"I'm sure. No cameras." The guard turned his head, and I had to force him to look back at me before anyone could read his lips.

"Where will you be after you finish eating?" I asked quickly, letting go of my spoon.

"I'll be watching the elevators on the second floor."

"Okay, great. Now forget we ever had this conversation, and if someone asks you to remember, say we talked only about the best combat techniques." I let my element slowly slip out of his head as I got to my feet. Tommy even gave me a dozy smile as I walked away. Now the only thing I had to do was break my tablet and find Tommy again.

Once I was back in my room, I took a seat in my uncomfortable metal chair. My tablet was on the desk, but I couldn't simply take it and smash it because the cameras would see me. Pulling my chair closer to the desk, I grabbed an empty glass and put it in front of me. Closing my eyes, I focused on my fire. I didn't remember anyone telling me I couldn't practice with my elements on my own.

When I opened my eyes again, flames danced across my palm, and I brought them closer to the glass. A moment later, my fire turned blue and I created a fireball, dropping it into the glass and watching the flames dance in it briefly before I extinguished them. Leaning my elbows on the desk, I stared at the wall for a while, fire flickering in my fingers.

I sighed, lowering my head on my arm and closing my eyes. I didn't know for how long I'd been like that, pretending I'd fallen asleep on my desk, my arm moving ever so slightly until it rested on the tablet. Focusing on my fire, I directed it to the tablet. The damn thing was resilient, and I had to increase my fire, but at least the fire's protective layer kept my arm unharmed.

Wrapping my whole body in a very thin layer of fire, I hoped the tablet wouldn't blow up and that Elemontera hadn't added any kind of protective magic in it. A loud crack made me open my eyes, and I jumped up, shaking my hands. The tablet's screen was slightly charred and lifted off the rest of the device. I swore, looking at my hands, praying that whoever was watching me would think I'd simply lost control of my element while I was dozing off. Such incidents were very rare, but it didn't mean they couldn't happen.

Picking up what was left of my ruined tablet, I cradled it to myself and went to find Tommy. He was exactly where he'd said he'd be, and his eyes regarded me curiously as I approached.

"Um, hey, do you know where I can get a new tablet?" I showed him the broken device with a sheepish grin on my face. "Mine is dead, I'm afraid."

"What happened?" Tommy's mouth fell open.

"It's embarrassing, actually. I closed my eyes for like a second and thought I was in the middle of a fight, used my fire, and then I woke up and..." I looked down at the tablet. "It was like this. Do you think you can help me?"

He waved at the other guard who was standing on the other end of the hallway. "Kevin, watch the elevator. I'll be right back." Then he looked back at me. "Come with me."

Once we were in the elevator, he pressed his bracelet against the small flashing screen instead of pressing a button. When the door finally opened, we entered into a white hallway with only three doors, which were also white. The only non-white thing was the light gray carpet. I couldn't see any cameras, just like Tommy had told me. Strange. What was the boss hiding in here that he didn't want anyone to see, including his security team?

"Go there to get yourself a new tablet." He pointed at the first white door to our left. "And don't forget to register it and sync it with your bracelet. You don't want to miss any important updates from the boss."

"Of course not." I offered him a wide smile, letting my air shoot out and find its way into his brain. "Actually, you'll get the tablet and wait for me here." I dumped the old tablet into his hands. He blinked at me, but obeyed.

I inched closer to the only door that was to the right, and noticed a keypad right next to it. "What's the code?" I yelled before Tommy could disappear into another room, my element quickly grasping his mind. He dictated the six-digit number to me, and I punched it in. The door clicked, and I pushed it open.

Chapter 9

My heart jumped all the way into my throat as I stepped inside, my hands shaking. The brightness in the room made me squint. The room wasn't bigger than my own, but the walls were padded and white. The tiles on the floor were completely white too. There wasn't any kind of furniture that I could see. Jaiden was sitting in the middle of the room, his knees drawn to his chest, his eyes tightly shut as he shook back and forth.

"Jaiden?" my voice was like a whisper. His eyes flew open, and I could see his forehead was covered in sweat, his dark eyes feverish.

"Now I'm hallucinating. Great," he said quietly. "Of course it would be you."

"It *is* me," I said, slowly inching closer. This room was seriously creeping me out, and suddenly I had a moment of realization. This was the room that had caused Jaiden's panic attacks.

"You're not real," he said, shaking his head.

"Jaiden, look at me." I crouched in front of him and placed my hand on his warm cheek. "Are you okay?"

He looked at me in shock, his hand closing over mine. "Moira? What the hell are you doing here?"

"I should be asking you the same thing. What is this... this room?" I glanced at the nearby wall, wrinkling my nose. Jaiden was wearing only a pair of white pants and white T-shirt, but he didn't look like he'd been harmed in any way. Well, if you didn't count the effect this room had on him.

"It's my nightmare," he said, pulling away from me. "You should go before someone sees you."

My eyebrows shot upward. "What are they doing to you?"

He tried to keep his face expressionless, but I could still see the tension in his body and the twitch of his mouth. "That's not your concern."

I groaned, unsure whether I wanted to strangle him or hug him. "Damn it, Jaiden. If you don't..." His hand suddenly shimmered and went nearly transparent. "What's going on with you?"

He pushed himself up, supporting himself on the wall, and turned away from me. "Just leave me, okay? You know where the lab is and you know I can't get you in there. You don't need me anymore," he said quietly, then looked at me over his shoulder. "Unless they're sending you on some mission...?"

"No, I don't need you. God, Jaiden! Just tell me what's happening to you! Is that so damn hard? Maybe I can..." I got to my feet.

"No. You have to go, and forget you ever saw anything."

"I can't. I won't!" I crossed my arms.

He faced me again, leaning his back against the wall. "I'm not like you. My elements... they're not like yours. You were born with them. I wasn't."

"What?" My eyebrows furrowed. "What do you mean you weren't born with them?" That didn't make any sense. Every person on the planet was born with an element, at least one, even if it was too weak to be used.

He swallowed, closing his eyes for a moment. "I mean... I was born like a regular elemental, not like you."

"But you said..."

"I lied. My father didn't find a way to manipulate an unborn child's genes before anyone else. He found a way to create a second element in me after I was born and enhance the power of both of my elements." This time his cheek became translucent for a moment.

"Okay, whatever." I was sure my mom would be freaking out right now and would want to know the details, but I didn't care whether his elements had come from regular genetic manipulations or from the moon. "But what's wrong with your elements now?"

"They're not really permanent. I need a serum to keep them strong or I won't be able to use them." He let himself slide back to the floor, his eyes fixed to the ground. "There, happy now? You do realize that if you say any of this to anyone, my father will kill you. So just go back to whatever you were doing and forget about this."

I just stared at him. "And why don't you just go get the damn serum instead of wasting time in this stupid room?"

He shot me an annoyed look. "Because my father is displeased with me and won't give it to me."

"So he'll just keep you in here until he needs you, is that it?" I put my hands on my hips, wishing I could just drag Jaiden out of this room, but if I did that, I'd put Lily's and my mission at risk. "Wait, this is your big secret. You actually sold Noah and me out back on the island because of this serum, didn't you? You were with the elementals for too long, and your father must have stopped giving you the serum when you didn't return soon enough. And all of this..." I waved my hands around. "You're letting him do all of this to you because of the stupid serum. Wow, Jaiden, wow."

"Look, I'm sorry about what happened to you and the others, but you don't know what it's like not to have elements. Without them, I'm nothing. Completely weak and useless." The pain in his eyes tore at my heart.

He was right; I didn't know what it was like for him. There were so many things that I believed I would have done differently if I were in his place, but his father had taught him that his only value was in his abilities. If I'd been listening to the same thing for years, maybe I'd get to believe it too.

"That's not true," I said matter-of-factly, not willing to walk away without at least trying to make him see my way. "There's nothing weak about you, Jaiden, even without your elements."

"What do you want from me?" His eyes bored into mine, as if trying to see through me. "Everyone, including you, always needs something from me... either my protection, my abilities, information... Do you think any tainted elementals like Noah and the others would have followed me if I had offered them nothing? Would I even be here now if you hadn't needed me to show you where the lab was?"

I closed my eyes for a moment. Whatever I told him, he'd find a way to convince me and himself that I was either lying or wrong. Steeling myself and wiping any emotion off my face, I took a deep breath.

"You want to keep sitting here and be your father's slave for the rest of your life? Fine. Be my guest. It's not like I can't do everything on my own. But if you really want that serum and your elements back, you're going to knock out the guard when he comes here next time. It's not like you can't fight without your elements and it's not like he's going to seriously injure his boss's son. If you're successful please come find me so we can have a drink. If not, well at least you tried." Without another word, I turned on my heel and strode out of the room, my shoulders tense.

As the door closed behind me, I slumped against it until I saw the confused expression on Tommy's face. Regaining my composure, I pushed myself to my feet, my air sneaking into his head again. "Do you know the code for that last door?"

"Yes," he said.

"Great. Then why don't you tell me?"

I'd left Tommy outside the door to keep watch and ended up in a small room full of vials and papers. It looked almost like a small lab. There was another door, but I didn't see a way to open it, so I focused on what I had in front of me.

A rack of vials filled with colorful liquids caught my eye, and I went closer to inspect it. Careful not to break anything, I lifted one of the vials and saw a sticker with a name on it: Amber. Huh, what could that mean? I picked another vial and found more names, such as George, Kevin, and Tina. I assumed those were names of people, and not of the liquids.

One of the vials was crimson and completely different from the others, so I picked it up. Jaiden's name was taped to it. My pulse sped up. Was that the serum Jaiden needed? If so, there was only one vial like that here, no more. Maybe the boss had already prepared it and left it here until he decided to give it to Jaiden.

I looked around until I found two empty vials. Popping the cork very slowly, I poured a couple of drops of the liquid into the empty vial. Closing everything again, I hoped no one would notice someone had touched the vials. I pocketed the one with the drops. Getting back to the desk, I rummaged through the things on it until I found a stack of papers with photographs and profiles of people.

I didn't recognize any of the faces until my eyes fell on an envelope with Jaiden's name. I opened it and found what looked like a birth certificate, with the "Mother's name" field empty. The next paper stated that an experiment on him had started when he was only three months old. I skimmed through the rest of the papers with information about things I couldn't even begin to understand—until I saw the last sentence, which stated: "The first semi-successful experiment; supplement needed."

I was about to return the papers into the envelope when I noticed a bunch of photographs inside. What I saw made my stomach turn upside down. I held up a photo of a crying baby, its tiny body full of IV needles and connected to some machines. The next photo was of the same baby surrounded by fire. The next one was a scan of elemental energy, and results of a bunch of tests. I tucked everything back the way I'd found it, although I doubted anyone would notice something had changed in this mess.

The other files seemed to be all about experiments, but who were all these people? Some of them weren't young, so I didn't quite understand why Jaiden's file was with theirs. As I flipped through other files, a familiar face caught my eye. The guy Jaiden had shot in that alley. The one who had looked too old to be one of us.

I checked the info, and indeed he was four years older than me. At the bottom of his file, in huge black letters, it was written, "Volunteer." Did that mean he'd volunteered to have his elements enhanced? But how? When I turned the paper, I saw that under, "Cause of death," it stated that he'd been killed in the field. There wasn't anything that could tell me when or where these experiments had taken place or what they consisted of.

The guy had been older and he could turn into air. Did that mean Elemontera had found a way to transform older elementals into tainted elementals? I went back to other files, checking the cause of death. On most of them it said death had occurred a couple of days after the experiment because the body was too weak to handle the tainted elements. Only one of them had managed to last longer than a week.

Oh, God. They were all failed experiments, which meant Elemontera was still trying to find a way to enhance elements so regular elementals could become like us. Jaiden was their only mostly successful experiment, but they didn't need to enhance a baby's elements. They wanted to do it with adults; adults who'd pay great money for it. If they'd succeeded, would Elemontera have stopped hunting tainted elementals? Did the government even know about this?

I took one of the papers and tucked it into my pocket. One paper could easily disappear in here and it was totally random, so even if someone noticed it was missing, it wouldn't look suspicious. I just had to make sure no one caught me with it. Arranging everything to look more or less how it'd been before I touched it, I cursed myself for not knowing more about these things.

Someone like my mom would probably be able to tell what was going on just by looking at the strange medical terms that were pretty much everywhere. She might even be able to recognize what was in that vial. I just had to get it to her.

Tommy was still obediently waiting for me when I got out. "Why did the boss give you the code for this room?" I couldn't imagine he'd let many people inside, especially when he was obviously so intent on keeping this secret that there weren't even any cameras.

"So I can give Jaiden his medicine," Tommy simply said.

"Why does the boss trust you so much?"

"I'm his distant relative and I'm loyal to him."

"Ah, wonderful." I, or maybe my air, briefly toyed with the idea of removing one of the boss's most loyal men, but I couldn't let that happen. Instead, I snatched the new tablet from Tommy's hands. "You won't remember any of this happened. And if someone asks, I was here to replace my tablet and nothing more. Nothing out of the ordinary happened."

He blinked as I released his mind, and laughed. "Try not to break this one."

I cradled the tablet to myself as we walked to the elevator. "I won't. Promise. Thank you so much."

As we went back to the main floor, I hoped I'd see Jaiden again very soon. But now I had to figure out how to take the vial and the paper I'd stolen to my mom. I wondered if the government knew about these experiments. It wouldn't surprise me if they did. Until they could have what tainted elementals had, they were willing to hide us and hunt us all down in fear for their safety, or more like out of fear of losing the power. But if by some miracle they could become like us, that would be another story.

Chapter 10

The next day a guard entered my room, and my breath got stuck in my chest. Had they discovered something unusual? Had they somehow found out what I'd done yesterday?

"Can't you at least knock?" I glared at him, my voice quivering only a little. My body perfectly still, I didn't dare get off the bed, because I wasn't sure my legs would be able to support me.

The guard approached me, some kind of a device in his hand. "I've come to upgrade your bracelet a little since your elemental energy seems to have spiked up."

"Oh." I extended my arm so he could press the device against the bracelet. Damn it. This was probably a consequence of my little accident with the tablet. They clearly didn't want me to ruin all their inventory. The device beeped, and the guard flashed me a smile. "All done."

After he left, I glanced at my bracelet. I could still feel my elements and reach out with them, so they hadn't blocked them. But maybe someone would block my elements if they saw me sleeping. Hopefully, I wouldn't have to do any more stupid things to reach my goal. Slipping into my sneakers, I jumped off the bed.

As I made my way down the hallway, I nearly bumped into a group of guards who were dragging two teenagers with them. The captives were struggling, crying, and screaming, but the guards ignored them. Were they new recruits or new lab rats? Bile rose in my throat when I thought of how Elemontera was finding *volunteers* for their experiments. But there was nothing I could do right now to help those teens. I couldn't stop Elemontera. Not until I found a way into the main lab.

Someone's hand grabbed my arm, sending shivers down my spine. I yelped, turning around, and found myself face to face with Jaiden, who smirked at me.

"Did you miss me?" he asked.

I grinned at him and wrapped my arms around him, glad that he was here and not in that damn room. His hand wound up in my hair as I tried to pull back, and suddenly we were so close that I could have brushed my lips against his if I'd wanted to. I looked up into his dark eyes, and we just stared at each other for a moment. I rested my hands on his chest as his arms hugged my waist.

"Oh, God," a guard groaned as he saw the two of us, and we jumped apart. I licked my dry lips, looking away.

"We should go somewhere else," Jaiden said.

"Yeah." I couldn't agree more. I couldn't even speak to him in this place with eyes and ears everywhere. That was so incredibly frustrating, and yet another reason to destroy the damn place forever. My elements surged again and I had to shove them back.

"Let's go." Jaiden started down the hallway and I followed him to the elevator. He pressed the button for the rooftop and I arched an eyebrow, but he just smiled at me. When we walked outside, I was blinded by the morning sun. The rooftop was empty, and the fresh breeze ruffled my hair. I breathed in, my shoulders finally relaxing. But when I opened my mouth to say something, Jaiden put a finger in front of his lips and shook his head. Elemontera could still hear us. Great.

"Why didn't I know that I had access to the rooftop?" I frowned, realizing the alarm hadn't beeped when I crossed through the door, and I knew Jaiden hadn't done anything to disable it or grant me access. And we weren't on a mission, so we couldn't have automatic permission.

"Because no one remembered to tell you." His eyes sparkled with amusement.

I groaned. "Where else can I go?"

"I'm afraid not anywhere far, but you can see it all on your tablet. If you still have it." A ghost of a smile traced his lips. "If you don't mess up your next mission, you might even get your first free day."

"Wow, progress!" I clapped my hands in excitement that I didn't really feel. Maybe some idiot in Elemontera would misinterpret my words and conclude I was Elemontera's most enthusiastic agent. Jaiden offered me his hand and I took it.

We walked to the edge of the roof. The city was bathed in golden rays of sunshine, the windows glistening, people milling around. Jaiden let go of me, and I placed my hands on the low stone wall, looking over the city. He came to stand behind my back and wrapped his arms around me.

"Your energy is spiking way too much," he whispered into my ear. "I could teach you something. A favor for the favor you did to me."

"Okay," I said, digging my fingers into the cold stone as Jaiden traced his fingers down my neck. He pushed me forward so I was trapped between him and the wall, my breathing leaving my lips in a sigh, my whole body tingling.

"Look down," he said, his breath tickling my neck. "Pick whoever you want. Get inside their head. Make them do whatever you want."

"How is that going to help?" I tried to turn my head to look at him, but I couldn't. His grip on me was too strong and tight. My element almost jumped out of me from impatience, as if it were mad at me for stalling and asking dumb questions.

"You'll see." He nuzzled my neck. Taking a deep breath, I focused on my air, and a shimmering thread rose from my hand, traveling down toward the person I could barely see. And yet, I could feel the exact moment my element entered his brain. I ordered the man to walk back a few steps and then continue on his way as if nothing had happened. I laughed as some woman looked at the man, probably surprised by his actions. God, this felt good.

"Now reach out for someone's mind, get inside and get out."

"Um, okay." I shoved my element inside a woman's mind, weaving around the brain signals, and pulled my element back. "Will you now tell me what the point of this was?"

"Don't be impatient." He chuckled, his right hand tracing circles over my stomach.

"If someone told you I was a patient woman, they lied." I leaned into him, raising my hand so I could reach behind me and touch his face, but his fingers wrapped around my wrist, holding my hand in front of me.

"Pretend you're going to reach into someone's mind, but instead wrap your element around your arm."

I tried to do what he wanted me to, but instead of my air, fire coated my fingers. Letting out a frustrated sigh, I pulled back the fire and let my air out, picturing a person standing not far from me. A shimmering thread hovered above my hand, as if unsure where its target was.

"Good," Jaiden said. "Guide it to your hand."

I dragged my air toward me, but as soon as it reached my skin, it slipped inside of me and was gone. "Is there are point to this or you're just trying to drive me crazy?"

"Try it again," he said with a soft laugh.

"Fine." I pouted, focusing on my element again. This time the shimmering thread wrapped itself around my fingers until my whole hand looked like a shimmering glove.

"Hold it like that."

I did as he asked, looking at my hand until I could no longer see the shimmering, but I could still feel my element right where it was. "What just happened?"

"You just learned how to use up a bit of that energy that causes the spikes, and when you hold it like that, the detectors don't notice how powerful it really is. If you do this whenever you feel like your elements want to rip their way out of you, you might get them to calm down easier."

I pushed the element back, and it settled inside of me, calmer than before. "Nice. Thank you."

His lips brushed my cheek. "No. Thank *you*."

"What about the shimmering? How do I hide that?" If there was a way to do that, other tainted elementals would be able to see what I was doing while I was mind-controlling someone.

"You can't. Many tainted elementals can't see the shimmering when it goes for them, and it's unlikely someone else will see it during mind control anyway. Just try to make your element as thin as possible without breaking the contact." Jaiden stepped back, the cold breeze hitting my back as he let go of me. "Let's go before they send someone to find us."

"Yeah, good idea." It would be a shame if my special access privileges got revoked before I even got to properly use them.

Chapter 11

"Finally," Tommy said as he saw Jaiden and me getting out of the elevator, relief flashing across his face. "You both need to prepare for a mission. Now!"

"Why? What happened?" Jaiden asked.

"The tainted elementals we've been looking for have been located. We should hurry before they get a chance to escape again." Tommy ran off down the hallway before I could ask him what he meant by tainted elementals. Elemontera was always trying to catch tainted elementals, and I had no clue which ones they had found this time.

"Do you think it's those elementals that attacked us at the university?" I looked at Jaiden, my throat constricting at the thought that Elemontera had found Noah and the others before they could leave the city. They should have already gone to Roivenna, but I couldn't contact them to find out if things had gone like planned.

He shrugged. "Let's find out. Get ready and meet me here." He strode back to the elevator, and I headed for my room.

I put on a black shirt, black leather jacket and a pair of black pants with numerous hidden pockets, and I managed to stuff the vial and the paper I'd stolen in one of them. Then I picked up my tablet to check if someone had sent me info about the mission. A map flashed on the screen, and I saw our target was a building in an industrial part of the city.

Some of the photographs taken by a satellite showed images of the building, which had dilapidated walls and a broken sign on it that said *Chip Factory*. There weren't any photographs of people, but that wasn't surprising considering we were looking for elementals who could turn into air. Another image showed high levels of elemental energy, which meant one of Elemontera's agents must have already investigated the place.

Although high energy levels weren't really a confirmation of anything, because they could have been caused by a fight with elements or any other activity that involved lots of energy. The goal of our mission was to capture the elementals or kill them if they resisted. Relief overcame me when I saw Raven's face on a photograph, which meant we'd be going after the elementals that had attacked us at the university and not one of our friends.

It appeared that Raven's family owned the building, and her real name was Sandy Carter. Elemontera hadn't identified any of those with her, but there were at least five of them. The alarm sounded, indicating that it was time to go, so I didn't have time to read whatever Elemontera had found out about Raven's family. Shutting down the tablet, I threw it on the desk and hurried to meet with Jaiden and the other agents.

"The team will storm the building, and if the elementals are still there, they'll try to escape, so you and I will wait outside and try to spot any shimmering, okay?" Jaiden said as we materialized on top of a building across from the one where elementals were supposedly hiding.

I nodded. "I doubt they're still here. They could have already escaped through some tiny hole that we don't know about."

"Doesn't matter," Jaiden said. "You watch the front, and I'll watch the back. The bracelet is set up to beep if you get close to me so you don't mistake me for our targets." Turning into air, he flew away.

I waited until the shimmering cloud vanished behind the oak trees and rooftops. Elemontera's mission could go to hell for all I cared, so I made sure I was alone and turned into air, flying to the nearest alley. I looked around, pretending I'd seen something, and looked up straight into the camera. Elemontera could probably see me too, but they wouldn't be able to tell if I'd seen something shimmering or not.

I just hoped someone from Lily's team was watching, too, and that Noah was somewhere close. Turning invisible again, I lifted into the air and climbed on a rooftop. Shouts sounded from the street as Elemontera's agents blew up the front door and rushed into the building.

I couldn't see any shimmering anywhere, but that didn't mean the rogue elementals weren't trying to escape. Maybe they were flying low around the building or had found a sewer or something. Elemontera's team had brought various devices to try to block all the exits, but I didn't know how effective that would be. I assumed we'd find out soon enough.

A couple of minutes passed, and I jumped from foot to foot, wondering if Noah would come. When I turned around, I noticed a shimmering cloud coming my way. Bracing myself for a fight in case it was the enemy, I waited for the cloud to reach the rooftop. The cloud transformed into a familiar boy with blue eyes and black hair.

"Noah! You almost scared me." I breathed out a sigh of relief. Glancing around us, I reached with my air just to see if I could touch someone's mind, but found nothing.

"I'm glad you're okay." He pulled me into a tight hug. "I assume you have something for me."

"Yeah." I bent down on one knee and dug out the vial and the paper. "Do you have a pen and a piece of paper?"

"Um." Noah rummaged through the pockets of his dark blue jeans. "Lucky for you, I do."

"Thanks." I took the paper and scribbled a message on it, along with the address I'd found in Sheridan's office. "You'll deliver this to my mom, and no one else will find out about it." Without a second thought, my air shot out, making Noah grimace in pain as it tore through his defenses.

"Moira? Stop!" he yelled through gritted teeth.

"I'm sorry," I said, but my voice was distant. "I don't want anyone to see or read this message, and that includes you. You won't tell Lily, and you won't tell anyone else under any circumstances about the note or the vial. And you won't try to find a way to let them know I mind-controlled you. You'll tell Lily that I found the lab, but that I need to find a way to get inside first. Tell her that Elemontera is trying to convert regular elementals into tainted elementals, and it would be great if she could check if the government is financing that project, too."

Noah's nostrils flared, his fists clenched. "Get out of my head."

"Of course." I let my element slip out, and I could swear it felt as if it couldn't be happier.

"You didn't have to do this! You should trust me!" Noah yelled. "What the fuck is wrong with you?"

"You should go now. I have work to do." The corners of my lips quirked up. Somewhere deep inside of me, I knew that this was a wrong thing to do to a friend, but my element silenced those doubts very quickly. Noah would get over it. And if he didn't, Lily would send someone else.

He shot me an indignant look before he pocketed the vial and the papers and turned into air. When he was out of sight, I noticed shimmering in another alley that wasn't far from the building that was swarming with Elemontera agents.

Turning into air, I plunged toward the shimmering, but it disappeared from view. Taking corporeal form again in an abandoned alley, I carefully picked my way through the trash and broken glass. If the broken window was of any indication, someone must have been here. Had the elementals tried to escape through it?

As I slowly approached the window to peer inside, something hit me in the back of the head. I swayed on my feet, and all I could see was a blurry silhouette of a man. Another blow came from behind, sending me sprawling to the ground. My face ended up in the dirt, and I coughed. Rolling over, I saw four men coming toward me, guns in their hands. Finding my air inside of me, I whipped them with it, knocking their guns away. The men squinted at me, shielding their eyes from the wind I'd created, while I struggled to get to my feet.

But almost an instant later, my wind was met with another air attack, and I had no clue which one of the men was an air elemental. Turning my fists into fire that was half blue, half red, I hit the ground and sent the fire toward them, trying to block their path. A wave of water extinguished my fire, and I immediately called to my air so I could reach for the men's minds. But before my shimmering thread could reach them, the ground shook underneath me and vines shot out of the dirt, entwining themselves around my legs. Burning them with my fire, I tried to free myself, but I couldn't use both air and fire at the same time.

"Who are you? What do you want?" I yelled, although I doubted that would distract them. They were all older, over thirty, so they couldn't be tainted elementals, unless someone had succeeded in what Elemontera couldn't have done.

"You," one of the men said, pushing his black hair out of his light blue eyes, and grabbed the gun off the ground, firing at me. I only had a moment to kick off the burning vines and deflect the bullets with my air. As the bullets returned toward the rest of the men, they used their own elements to stop them. Raising a wall of fire, I backed down the alley, wondering where my backup was and what on earth these men could possibly want from me.

Had someone been spreading the word about tainted elementals and now someone wanted to capture one as proof? Yeah, right, as if that would help them. If the government didn't want anyone to know, they'd simply dismiss the whole thing as a hoax, and there was nothing anyone could do aside mind-control hundreds of people to believe in what they couldn't really see or feel.

My firewall was torn down a second later, and I immediately sent out my air to grasp the men's minds. It was very easy to get inside. "St..." I couldn't finish my order because I was knocked down to the ground. A bald man with wide hazel eyes slammed his fist into my face. A wave of pain erupted through my whole body, and I was glad he'd missed my nose or he'd have broken it.

As he tried to pin me to the ground, my air rose inside of me like a snake, slithering into the guy's mind. There was only one thing I wanted to do.

Kill them all.

It was like a whisper in the wind, but I obeyed it. Shoving my element in between the brain signals, I crushed them, leaving nothing behind. My attacker's eyes went wide, and he fell off me. Before the others could even begin to comprehend what was going on with their friend, I forced my element into their heads until they all dropped to the ground around me.

Breathing hard, my legs wobbly, I looked at the dead bodies around me with strange detachment. Lifting my eyes, I thought I could see a shimmering cloud, which disappeared a second later. Someone had been watching me.

"Moira!" Jaiden's voice full of worry broke through my thoughts, and I turned to look at him. He rushed toward me, placing his hand on my cheek, and I winced. His fingers came away with blood, and I suspected I had a nasty cut on my face.

"Are you okay? What...?" Jaiden's eyes fell on the men, and his lips parted in surprise. "What did you do?"

"I..." I ran a hand through my hair, my fingers getting stuck in the muddy knots. Two more Elemontera agents ran toward us, their faces paling at the sight of the bodies.

"Send the investigators. I want to know who these people are," Jaiden said. The men nodded and went away.

"We're going to tell them I did this, okay?" Jaiden grabbed me by the shoulders, looking straight into my eyes. "Good thing there aren't any cameras here."

But even if there were cameras, no one would be able to prove that Jaiden couldn't have killed the men from a distance. I nodded at him, my head hurting. Actually, every inch of my body ached.

"What did they want?" he asked.

"I don't know. They just attacked me and I..."

"Why didn't you interrogate them first?" he hissed.

"I wasn't thinking clearly. Sorry." I didn't want to tell him that at that moment there hadn't been any coherent thought on my mind aside from the urge to kill. My element had been the one controlling me, or had it all been me?

"We'll find out." He sighed, pulling me into his arms. The investigators found their way to us and crouched near the bodies, inspecting them with their devices. Jaiden guided me farther from them.

"Did you catch the elementals?" I asked.

"No. The building was empty when the team got there, and I didn't see any shimmering."

"I think I saw one of them watching me fight the men, but... I don't know. I..." At this point, I wasn't even sure I could trust my own eyes.

"Shh, don't say anything. You're still shaken from the fight." He led me to the front steps of a nearby building, and we sat down.

I stared down at my hands in my lap, wondering if this meant that I could lose control of my elements and turn into a killer; into a real monster. No, Jaiden was right. I was still agitated after what happened. I wasn't thinking straight. Maybe I just needed some time.

Chapter 12

I had no idea how long Jaiden and I had been sitting on the stairs while the investigators did their job. A woman with long blonde hair tied in a ponytail approached us, her face serious.

"These four men were magic disease carriers. The cops have been looking for them for months. They all have huge criminal records, and it seems they'd been stealing elements from their victims," she said, rubbing her neck.

"Carriers?" I frowned. "Carriers can't sense my elements. Why would they come after me?"

"I don't know," the woman said. "We suspect someone hired them to attack you."

Jaiden and I looked at each other, and then Jaiden nodded at the woman. "Send the report to the boss."

She trudged off, and I faced Jaiden. "Do you think the elementals hired those carriers to kill me? But how would they know...? They knew we were coming, didn't they? It was a set-up."

"Yeah, looks like it," Jaiden said. "They must have tipped off one of our agents so we'd come here looking for them."

"But why would they send carriers after me? They couldn't have known I'd be alone. And why would they risk attacking someone much stronger than them?"

"Maybe they're hired assassins. Some carriers still accept kill jobs to get money and elements. Not everyone gets to obtain an element legally or knows how to control himself. Maybe the elementals lied about you and thought you'd be caught unawares. You know they want to kill us all. They've already tried. Maybe they thought you'd underestimate the threat. Or it was all a distraction so they could escape, and you happened to be the one to run into the men."

I shook my head. "But carriers weren't surprised that they couldn't feel my elements." They were a bit stupefied when one of them dropped dead, but that was a different thing. "So they must have known at least something about what they were dealing with. If the elementals had simply told them we had some special kind of a blocking bracelet, then they would be surprised to see I have two elements." My whole face throbbed as I spoke, my cheek feeling as if it had doubled in size. "Unless they would have attacked anyone for the right sum of money because they already had elements in their system."

"Or they were mind-controlled to attack you. We know at least one of the elementals has that ability," Jaiden said. "But out of all people, they picked assassins, not some random guys, so they must have gone through some trouble to find them and maybe even offered some money to lure them in. We should look into it, because these assassins can't just be found on the street, even with our special abilities."

Part of me was immensely glad that the men had been assassins and not innocent people. I'd have never forgiven myself otherwise. "God, they can turn anyone into a criminal. Force people to do things they'd never do. We have to stop them."

"We do. Finding Raven's family is our best chance, but they all seem to have taken their possessions and vanished. Maybe they're in another city or country by now."

"But Raven is still here. What do you know about her?"

"Not much. Her family used to own one of the biggest factories of nanochips, but it was closed down after Raven's grandfather died. They had a big house for the whole family, and they had enough money to live comfortably. Raven was an excellent student in high school, but she never went to college. Actually, she just disappeared. There's no evidence that anyone knew she had more than one element."

"She must have discovered her other elements and realized she couldn't have a normal life," I said. "Someone must have found her. Hasn't anyone seen her? Tracked her on surveillance cameras? Through a friend?"

"Actually, the techs didn't find any trace of her on any footage, but she could have stayed in parts of the city that aren't monitored that much. No one has seen her since high school and her old friends have no clue where she is or why she left."

"Do they have memory gaps? She might have mind-controlled them, and I could fix that," I said, my element stirring happily at the thought that it could be in someone's head again.

"No, I don't think so. She was probably hiding or avoiding everyone."

"What about the building? Any clues in there? Fingerprints?" I asked hopefully.

"No idea yet." Jaiden got to his feet, offering me a hand. "Do you want to come see how the investigators are doing in there?"

"Sure." Maybe I could take a look and see if I could find anything useful.

When I entered a brightly lit room, one of the investigators cringed as he saw my face, but I ignored him.

"What is all this?" I asked as I took in the room. A huge table stood in the middle, filled with papers and books. One of the walls was covered with a huge map, various photographs, and bits and pieces from books and newspapers. There was also a huge hand-drawn circle divided into four parts, representing each of the main elements. Actually, the whole room was filled with papers, books, and notebooks.

"I've no idea," Jaiden said, frowning as he picked up a sheet of paper.

"Oh, it's safe to touch things. We got the prints already." One of the investigators rolled her eyes at him.

He flashed her a smile. "Sorry. Forgot to ask. So, did you get the prints?"

"We did." Her shoulders slumped. "But we couldn't find a match in our system or anywhere else. It's like these people don't even exist."

"But we know they do, so go on. Find their DNA or something." Jaiden waved her off, and she glared at him as she crossed to the other side of the room where the others were gathered around an old couch.

"If this was a set-up, then that means the elementals wanted us to see this. I mean, why leave all of this here?" I picked up one heavy book with a dirty yellowish cover to check the title, cringing. "*The History of Magic*. Huh." I dropped the book and read the other titles that I could see. "*Myths of Elements, Elements Revealed, The Great Prophecies*. Um, okay, sounds a lot like they were researching elements."

Jaiden got closer to the wall, carefully examining the sticky notes and newspaper article cutouts. "Do you remember this?" He pointed at one small yellow paper. "The hero, the strong, and the murderer shall meet. One path they all must choose or the elements shall swallow the earth."

"Oh, God." I groaned. "That silly thing? I think I read it… in that book you had on Roivenna?"

"Yeah." He tapped another paper as I came closer. "This apparently says there's a way to become the hero."

"Does it include saving the planet or something?" I chuckled, studying various articles in all of which the word *hero* had been highlighted with a yellow marker.

"Maybe." Jaiden's brows drew together in a frown.

"It looks as if they went through tons of books on elements and prophecies, and cut out everything that mentions the hero, whoever he is." In some instances, it seemed as if the hero was a specific person, the chosen one. But in others, it was used more like a metaphor. Not that I believed in any of that shit.

"It could be some kind of a message. They wouldn't just leave all of this here if they didn't want something." Jaiden ripped two papers off the wall and handed them to me. "Check this out. The hero doesn't sound like a savior."

I took the papers and skimmed over the text. "Um, it says the hero is supposed to gain control over all elements and sub-elements. What the hell?" I went back to the table and dropped the papers on it. "This is insane. All of it. If there's a message in any of this, I'm not getting it. Unless this is their way of showing us they think they're more powerful than us. Maybe they worship this hero or whatever."

Jaiden leafed through one of the books. "I think there's a prophecy about this somewhere. I heard it long time ago. Let's see if I can find it."

"I still don't think that will help us." I flipped through the papers and looked underneath the books, trying to find a hidden note or at least something that made sense. I turned to Jaiden, who was still trying to find the prophecy. "Are there any cults that share these beliefs? Maybe we could track the elementals through that. If they went to one of those meetings and became obsessed with crazy made-up stuff, then maybe someone will recognize them."

Jaiden's gaze flipped upward. "Oh, there are plenty, but you know how they are, all secretive. I'm sure they wouldn't know any names or any personal info. Not to mention it would take us ages to track them all down and mind-control them to answer our questions."

"So, do you have any clue how to become this special wielder of all elements and sub-elements?" I grinned and immediately winced as every muscle in my face protested. "Or maybe the elementals left this here so we can bang our heads against the wall trying to figure out what this means, when in fact it means nothing and they're just wasting our time?"

"There's a merging ritual, and then the merged elements should show the location of sacred artifacts on a map... I've no clue how. Anyway, once the artifacts are retrieved, the hero has to go through some trials, and if he passes, he will gain control over all elements and be the most powerful person on the planet."

"Sounds like every boring prophecy ever. Let's get out of here, and the rest of the team can deal with this." I was sure we'd been sent to capture elementals, not to figure out why someone was crazy enough to think one person should have all the power and be the most special.

Jaiden dropped the book on the table. "Good idea. You should get cleaned up. That cut on your face could get infected."

"Yeah, I think I'm going to need some help with that." I gave him a pointed look, and we started for the door. There were some things I needed to discuss with him without too many prying ears.

"We should go…" he started to say when one of the agents blocked our path.

"You have to report to the headquarters immediately," the agent said.

Jaiden muttered a curse and I rolled my eyes.

"Guess we'll have to talk in the air," he said. "Do you need help?"

"No, I'll be fine." My element wasn't drained or tired, just satisfied. "Wait, is my face going to hurt even worse if I turn into air?"

Jaiden grimaced. "Yep."

Why had I even asked? Bracing myself, I let my body turn into air. The pain intensified, but I could fly just fine. Still, Jaiden's idea to talk while we were in the air would have to wait for another time because I was sure it would hurt, even though I couldn't understand how my face still felt normal when I was a shimmering cloud.

Surging through the air that cooled my invisible swollen cheek, I wondered if the elementals would try to get inside Elemontera while many of the agents were out. I hoped there wouldn't be a surprise waiting for us when got back, because I'd hate to see them ruin my mission.

It turned out the only person waiting for us at Elemontera was the boss. We were ushered into his office before I could even see my face. If the strange looks people had given me as I passed them by were of any indication, maybe I was better off without a mirror.

The boss's back was turned to us as the door of his office snapped shut. When he finally faced us, his eyebrows went up at the sight of me, but his lips remained pressed into a tight line.

"What is so important that it couldn't wait?" Jaiden said, folding his arms.

"What is…" the boss spat out, his face flushed. "What is so important, you ask? These elementals have made a mockery out of our organization! I sent you to *capture* them!"

"Yeah, and that was what we were trying to do, but they were long gone when we arrived," Jaiden said calmly.

The boss observed him for a while, then scratched his chin. "And what caused all the spikes of elemental energy nearby? They were strong enough to be picked up by our detectors."

"Didn't they tell you? We were attacked by four magic disease carriers, hired assassins. I took them out," Jaiden said.

"You took them out?" An unidentifiable emotion flashed through the boss's eyes. "Ah, so that's what my informant meant when he said there had been complications. What were those men after?"

"No idea." Jaiden shrugged. "I didn't bother to ask. We were after the tainted elementals, not carriers. They were of no use to anyone."

His father gaped at him. "You should have consulted me first!"

"Oh, I would've asked, but you weren't there." Jaiden bit out, and I held my breath as the boss's eyes went wide. He came to stand in front of Jaiden until they were face to face, but Jaiden didn't even flinch, just glared at his father, his jaw set.

"Today's events must have messed with your head, boy," the boss said, stepping away. "We'll talk another time. Now go to your room. You're dismissed."

"I will if you let Moira come with me."

My heart skipped a beat, my skin tingling. The boss's cold eyes raked over me, his lip curling in disgust. "Fine," he waved his hand, and reached for his tablet. "But tomorrow you'll find those elementals and bring them to me."

"Yes, father." Jaiden took my hand and pulled me toward the door. When we were out in the hallway, I stopped, looking up at him.

"Are we really going...?" I wasn't sure if he'd been trying to push his father's buttons or if he'd been serious.

"Yeah." He flashed me a smile, so I followed him to the elevator. Actually, going to his room was a wonderful idea. There shouldn't be any cameras, so we could talk about whatever we wanted. I'd been forbidden to even step on that floor again, but now that the boss had allowed it... A slow smile crept across my face.

Chapter 13

As we went through the door that led to his father's private office and the rooms, I couldn't help but think about that time when Jaiden had me pinned against the wall, his hot mouth against mine. Biting my lip, I focused on the hallway in front of me. We stopped in front of a dark blue door, and Jaiden pressed his bracelet against the lock until the green light appeared.

Pushing the door open, he stepped aside to let me pass. "Come on."

I entered the spacious room with dark blue walls and mostly black furniture. The main source of light was a bright lamp in the shape of a ball. The windows were made of thick dark glass and didn't look like they could be opened, and it was almost impossible to see the city through them. The middle of the room was occupied by a big double bed.

"Sit down," Jaiden said, and I settled myself on the edge of the soft bed. He went over to the big black closet, opening a drawer and taking out a box. Next to the closet was a large bookshelf filled with books.

"Can we talk in here?" I hoped there weren't any hidden cameras. It would be really twisted if the boss was spying on his son. Not that it would surprise me much if he were, though.

"Yeah. Why do you think I brought you all the way here?" He sat next to me and placed the box on the bed, flipping it open to reveal a medical kit.

"How did you do it? I thought your father would never let you bring me here."

Jaiden bit on his lip, dabbing some liquid on a piece of gauze. "He thinks I killed four people with my mind, and usually after I use that ability, I'm a little... unhinged. He thinks my behavior is a consequence of using my ability, so he allows me things he usually wouldn't. Maybe he's afraid I'll do something dangerous." He let out a soft laugh. "It was a gamble, really. I figured he would need me tomorrow, so..."

I looked at my hands in my lap, my throat tight. I'd used my air to take out four men and I hadn't felt a thing, except the pure joy of my element. "Do you really feel different after you...?"

"No, but I used to get drunk after those missions. My father never figured it out." Jaiden gently pressed the gauze to my cheek and I hissed in pain, making him grimace. "I'm sorry."

"It's okay." I kept still so he could clean the wound. "I don't think I feel anything, you know... just..."

"Hey, you don't have to feel bad about it. You did what you had to." He caressed my cheek, his eyes warm. After he tossed the bloodied gauze into the trash can, he picked up a tube, squeezing white cream onto his fingers. Pressing his fingers to my cheek, he gently rubbed the cream into my sensitive skin. "This will help with the bruise."

"Thanks." I glanced around, but didn't see a mirror anywhere.

"Take off your jacket and shirt," he said, wiping his fingers.

My eyebrows shot up.

"You have a bloody gash on your jacket."

"Oh." The constant throbbing in my face had made me forget about any other injuries I might have. I slipped out of my jacket and pulled my shirt over my head, careful not to let it touch my cheek. Jaiden got to his feet, and I did my best to ignore his intense gaze.

"Your elbow," he said, grabbing another gauze dressing and taking hold of my arm.

"It's just a scrape," I said, but he carefully cleaned it and put a bandage on it.

"There," he said with a satisfied smile. "All done."

"Can I put my shirt back on?" I gave him a look through my eyelashes, a smile spreading over my lips.

"If you wish." He picked up the box and put it back into the closet while I slipped my shirt on.

"Um, I wanted to ask you... Do you have any idea how to get into the lab? Maybe some secret entrance or...?" I got to my feet.

"That's why I brought you here. I have an idea, but I don't know if it will work." He leaned against the closet. "I don't want to work for Elemontera anymore. I'm done with this, with everything..."

"So is there another way to get inside?" I ran my fingers over one of the books on the shelf. "Maybe you could..."

"I can't help you, because my father won't let me anywhere near the lab. I guess he's afraid I'll somehow convince one of the scientists to work on the serum," he said. "But you... You might be able to get in."

"How?" I arched an eyebrow at him. Speaking of the serum, I hoped that its secret would soon be revealed. My mom would figure something out.

"We're supposed to be looking for those elementals, and I'm sure no one will find anything. That's why you could come up with some idea. I don't know... something that could help or something that the scientists didn't think of. Your mom..."

"My mom knows many things, yeah, but I'm not her. I'm clueless about things like that. What would I even say?

I'm sure they thought of everything already. They're professionals."

"But you only need to get inside, right?" Jaiden asked. "You don't even need to have a real theory. You just have to convince the guards to let you through. Once you're inside, you can come up with another story for the scientists. Tell them you came for something else."

"I could try, but if they figure it out too soon, then what?" I'd be in trouble and my mission would fail. We couldn't afford that.

"I'll get you out. You can say I forced you to do it so you could ask about the serum."

"Um, okay, let's say that works... that I somehow get inside and get what I want. What will you do when Elemontera is raided?" I cocked my head at him.

"I don't care about Elemontera. You can burn it to the ground if you wish. But there's one thing I want..." He came to stand in front of me, his face serious. "You don't touch my father, okay? I'll deal with him myself."

"Yeah, okay," I said, keeping my face expressionless, even though part of me knew that I was lying to him. His father was a threat that Lily wanted to eliminate, and I agreed with her. I knew that Jaiden wanted that serum, but I couldn't let his father escape. "I just want this to be over."

"I know."

My eyes fell on a laptop near his desk. "Do you have Internet connection here?"

"Yeah, but the traffic is monitored, so if you want to contact someone, you better not."

"No, that's not what I want. Maybe there's something we could use to really help find those elementals. Even after Elemontera is gone, I'm not sure they won't try to attack us or hurt someone. That cult stuff seriously freaks me out. What if they're planning something? Besides, it's easier to find all about those silly prophecies on the Net than go through tons of dusty books."

"Maybe that's why they left the books. Maybe there was nothing there they couldn't already find elsewhere." He shrugged. "But if you want to search for something, go ahead."

"Okay, let's see what I can find." I grinned.

Jaiden started up the laptop and carried it over to me. I sat on the bed cross-legged and took the laptop. Opening the Web browser, I clicked the button for search engine. Maybe this whole thing would be a waste of time, but I wanted to at least try to come up with something reasonable in case the guards decided not to let me into the lab.

Jaiden settled next to me, the bed shifting under his weight. I searched for prophecies about the hero and got pages upon pages of results. "Everyone seems to be writing about this. God, I wish I was writing a paper for college right now and not researching this just to find a bunch of crazy elementals."

But as I browsed the websites, something else caught my eye; a mention of the murderer from one of those stupid, nonsensical prophecies. I clicked on the link before I could stop myself. "On the day of the full moon, the murderer will kill four dark souls and begin the preparation for the trials of darkness." A shiver ran down my spine as I reread the text over and over again in my mind. "Um, this sounds... creepy."

Jaiden swore. "They sent those men at you because of this. Maybe they believe in it or they're just trying to scare you."

I swallowed past the lump in my throat. "I can't find anything about the trials."

"Forget about that. We need to *find* them, not join their cult." He took the laptop from me. "Let's see if there's a place where they could go. Maybe some holy ground or something."

"Where do you think they got all those books? They must have bought them, borrowed them or stolen them. If we could figure out where they've been... maybe some camera or something caught them at that place."

"It would be too late. Many people go to the libraries, and those elementals can make themselves invisible." Jaiden clicked through a couple of links. "Shit. It says that the location of sacred artifacts will appear only to the chosen one in a dream."

I rolled my eyes. "Does it say what idiot came up with this?"

"Nope. Apparently the first texts are at least a thousand years old." He kept scrolling through the pages.

"Wait!" I yelled as he scrolled past a news link. "What's that?"

Jaiden clicked on the headline. "Two precious books missing from the Museum of Magic. Two days ago. It is not known how the thieves got inside or how they managed to get their hands on the books. A witness says the books simply vanished."

"Is that museum somewhere in the west part of the city? I think I went there once in high school." I frowned.

"Yeah, I guess."

"Any other museums or libraries that have that type of book? We might not be able to figure out where the elementals were, but we could predict where they go next. Unless they've already robbed half of the city and no one in Elemontera noticed."

Jaiden handed me the laptop. "Actually, we can check that." He opened the drawer of the nightstand and took out his tablet. A couple of moments later, he lifted his eyes toward me. "The team tried this already, but the elementals either didn't go there, or the library was too full of people to do anything or try to monitor energy levels. So basically, it didn't work."

"Damn." I chewed on my fingernails. "Okay, so I can't walk into that lab saying I have a theory. If the guards can check what investigators have already done, like you can, they'll never let me in. Or worse, they'll tell me to ask the boss first."

Jaiden put down the tablet, nodding. "Yeah, they'd do that. You'd need to come up with something urgent that can't wait. Maybe while my father's out."

"And what if we dig out random scientific-sounding words and invent something? If they can't understand it..."

"They'd still ask you for the simple version."

I put the laptop next to me and lay down on the bed, groaning and closing my eyes. "God, I'm not smart enough to deal with this. The simplest thing I can come up with is to mind-control the hell out of the guards..." I opened my eyes and looked up at Jaiden. "I think I know how we're going to do this."

"How?" He climbed on the bed next to me, lying down on his side. "There are elemental energy detectors everywhere. And even if you risk it and get through the main door, the alarms will go off and the scientists will lock themselves in before you can even get to them."

"That's why we have to remove the detectors. They're technology. Technology malfunctions all the time." A slow smile was creeping over my lips, reinforcing the throbbing in my cheek, but I ignored it. "Is there a way to shut down the power?"

Jaiden considered it for a moment. "I'm afraid not. If the outside source of power fails, we have a generator which kicks in immediately. And the generator's wires are deep inside the walls and they are protected with magic. You can't get to them. My father made sure no one could attack the building from the inside. But those energy detectors are a recent addition and I've no clue how they're connected."

"Find out."

He sat up and reached for the tablet, his fingers moving swiftly over the screen. "I can't find anything. I guess we could ask someone, but it would be suspicious if the whole system shut down right after I asked."

"Is there a chance we could go on a patrol to look for elementals or something with someone who knows this stuff?"

"I don't know. Why?"

"I could mind-control them. Elemontera didn't protect the agents against me and they think I'm not stupid enough to try anything since my parents' lives are on the line. But I don't know if they'd send someone with such expertise on a regular patrol."

Jaiden shook his head. "They wouldn't. None of the regular agents know this. Only someone from the tech team could help."

I sighed. "Okay, do you know anyone from the tech team? A girl maybe?"

"Yeah," he said hesitantly. "But none of them particularly like me."

"Really? Did you sleep with all of them?"

"No!" he sneered. "Well, not *all* of them."

"Okay, so that was another terrible idea." The sole thought of some girl's hands on Jaiden made me want to cut through her brain with my element. Wow, okay. I took a deep breath.

I supposed I could try to mind-control one of them into thinking that the boss had ordered him to let me into the lab, just like I mind-controlled Tommy in the lunchroom, but even if I succeeded in getting a guard to a spot in Elemontera where I could use mind control, someone could see it, and it would be suspicious because they'd know there was no way that a guard got such an order. And mind-controlling all the guards one by one would take too much time and would be too complicated.

"I guess we're back to plan A," Jaiden said. "You have to convince the guards to let you in. I'm sure we'll be sent to look for elementals tomorrow, so we could go back to that building, find something, and ask to urgently speak with one of the scientists."

I looked at him, waving my hands in excitement. How hadn't I thought of this earlier? "The scientist! That's our key!"

He narrowed his eyes, tilting his head. "I don't follow. If you want to mind-control one of them, that will be complicated because they rarely go out alone, they use different hallways, and they definitely don't have the authority to invite agents into the lab without obtaining permission from my father."

"No, I wasn't thinking about them. Your father sent me once to take that biochemical weapon we'd found to some guy, Victor or something. I know where his lab is. If we are careful, we can catch him, and I can mind-control him to give us something that needs to go directly to the lab. Maybe something that is dangerous to put down. Something that would leave them with no choice but to let me into the lab." My lips spread into a smile. "I'd try it without involving Victor, but if I'm discovered before I get to the lab, then I'm screwed."

"I don't know anyone named Victor." Jaiden frowned. "Why would my father believe this guy sent him something? And how would he even find you?"

"I can say I was in the area and that he spotted me and... I don't know. I'll ask Victor if your father would believe it." I shrugged. "We can try. There's really nothing to lose."

He considered it for a moment. "Okay, we'll try that."

"Great. Now what?" I sat up, running a hand through my hair to untangle the knots.

"I don't know. Do you want to read a book? Watch a movie?"

"Movie would be good." I stretched my arms, fighting the urge to yawn.

Jaiden picked up the remote control and pressed a button. As I followed his gaze, I realized there was a plasma TV almost hidden on the dark wall.

"What would you like to watch?" he asked.

"I don't know. Anything." All I wanted to do was not move from the bed and get some rest. The screen went bright, the beginning of a movie flashing on it. Jaiden threw the remote on the bed and turned to me.

"Let's get you comfortable." He picked up the pillows and stacked them so I could lie down and still see the TV, and then he settled next to me. The movie seemed interesting, but it couldn't quite hold my attention. I kept glancing at Jaiden, who finally looked at me. There was something in his dark eyes, something warm and inviting.

I didn't waste another moment. Leaning forward, I pressed my lips against his. His mouth moved against mine, slowly and gently. When we pulled apart, we were both breathless.

"I…" he started to say, but I put my finger across his lips.

"Shh. Don't say anything." I pulled myself closer to him, resting my head on his shoulder, and closed my eyes.

Chapter 14

The next day Jaiden and I were called to the boss's office. The only thing he told us was to go out and find the elementals. That was exactly what we needed, so I hurried to take a shower and got dressed for a mission. Since the team was absolutely clueless about the possible location of the elementals, we'd been sent to patrol the city and report anything suspicious.

As I made my way to the elevator, I passed by a couple of agents, their faces grim. I wondered if they were worried because they couldn't catch the elementals or because we couldn't even discover the elementals' identities. Except for Raven's—or should I call her Sandy?

Jaiden was waiting for me when I emerged from the building, and I breathed in the fresh air, my face warmed by sunshine. Speaking of my face, whatever Jaiden had put on me yesterday had worked and my cheek wasn't swollen anymore, but a nice shade of purple had developed just under my eye. But as long as it didn't hurt like crazy, I'd live. I'd popped a painkiller just in case.

"You ready?" Jaiden asked, his hands in the pockets of his black leather jacket.

I nodded. "I hope this works." Turning into air, I rose up until I could see the whole city below me. Jaiden followed me, but soon he disappeared in another direction. I flew around a little because it would be too suspicious if I went directly in the direction of Victor's lab.

The city was alive with people and cars, and I wondered how many more elementals like me were in hiding or still didn't know they had an extra element. My generation was the first to have genetic manipulation go awry, but the same process had been repeated numerous times over the years.

I wondered why Elemontera or the government hadn't put a stop to the genetic manipulation if they were so against tainted elementals. But then again, our cases were rare, and still less magic disease carriers were being born, thanks to that process. Besides, if they planned to become like us, then they needed us so they could find a way to replicate our DNA or whatever it was that gave us an extra element.

Two hours later, I flew closer to that shop where Victor's lab was hidden. Landing in the nearby alley, I considered reaching all the way into the building and finding his mind. Focusing on my element, I let it roam, but as it brushed a mind, it slipped inside, snatching at the brain signals.

I gasped, unsure in whose mind I was inside, and tried to pull my element back, but it didn't work. My breathing ragged, I started running down the alley, as far as I could from that mind I was in. My element finally detached its greedy fingers and slammed into me, unsatisfied. I panted, leaning against the wall.

A shimmering not far from me caught my eye, and I stared at it, trying to figure out if it was a friend or enemy. If it was Jaiden, he would have already yelled something. I hadn't looked into any cameras or asked for a meeting with Noah, so it couldn't be him. Bracing myself for a fight, I waited for the shimmering to settle down. I couldn't exactly attack someone I didn't know without a reason, especially if it was some other elemental who thought I couldn't even see him.

When the shimmering cloud turned into a blue-eyed boy, I gritted my teeth and glared at him. "God, you could have said something! I almost attacked you!"

Noah approached me, his face serious, worry creasing his brow. "Hush. I came for you."

"What?" I gaped at him, stepping away as he took something out of the pocket of his brown coat. It was some kind of a white device that resembled a phone, but I was sure it wasn't one. "What is that?"

"Your mission has been compromised," he said, reaching for my arm. "I've been waiting for you to get outside so I could find you. Lily gave me this device so I can take off your bracelet and take you somewhere safe."

"What?" I blinked at him, a sour taste in my mouth. "Are my parents okay?"

"Yeah, they're fine, but Elemontera is about to find out that we sent agents to pretend to be your parents, so we have to get you out. Now!" He tried to take my wrist, but I pulled my hand away.

"You sent agents to pretend to be my parents?" I reached out with my element, but not for Noah's mind. I searched around to see how much time we had and if any other agents were around.

"We knew the boss would never accept that he doesn't know where your parents are when that's the only thing that keeps you loyal to Elemontera. He dispatched men to find your relatives too, no matter how distant."

I opened my mouth to say something, but he raised a finger to shush me.

"Don't worry. It's all been taken care of. Lily was afraid Jaiden had revealed something about your mission to his father, or that something had happened to you. You don't know how glad I am you're okay. But I don't know why the boss has issued this order now. Did you do something? Did he tell you anything?"

I chewed on the insides of my mouth. Oh, yeah. I had a pretty good idea why the boss had done it. After all, he wouldn't let just anyone go to his private floor and to his son's room. Now he needed to make sure he could control me. Maybe letting me go with Jaiden was a part of his plan to make me more compliant, because if I were to fall in love with his son, my loyalty would only be stronger, or that was what he could be thinking. "I... I don't know."

"Give me your hand," Noah said, his neck and shoulders tense, his eyes darting left and right. "We need to hurry!"

"No, I can't. I'm about to find a way to get inside the main lab."

"Didn't you hear a word of what I just said? Elemontera knows!" Noah hissed.

"We don't know that," I said calmly. "If they thought I was trying to do something, they would have already detained me and not let me out to give me a chance to escape."

"And what do you think they'll conclude when it turns out that people who are now living in your house are actually actors and not your parents?"

"Okay, so they'll find out. Maybe they'll think my parents are just smart and figured out they were monitored. They probably know my mom was friends with the ex-president of the Element Preservers. I mean, what did they expect, anyway? That they could monitor anyone and that no one would find out? Just because my parents went into hiding doesn't mean I had anything to do with it." I could always play dumb with Elemontera.

"Don't be crazy. You have to come with me. You could get yourself killed." Noah's eyes were pleading.

"And tell me when we're going to get a chance as good as this one? Will we let Elemontera hunt us forever because something *might* happen to me? I knew the risks when I signed up for this. You might think that what I'm doing is crazy or extremely stupid, but it's my life. And I won't back down now."

"Damn it, Moira!" Noah's face contorted with anger. "Think about it for a second. Just think about it!"

"I *am* thinking about it! And I'm not going anywhere, not now. Jaiden and I have a plan..."

"Jaiden?" Noah sneered. "Of course he's involved. I should have known. You want to get yourself killed, and for what? For him?"

"Look, it doesn't matter. I made my choice. You don't have to like it or agree with it." I moved my bracelet away so he wouldn't try to take it off by force.

"Great. Are you going to mind-control me like last time? What was so important about that note that you didn't want anyone to see?" His voice was cold as ice.

"Just forget it." I shook my head and started down the street.

"We found out what you did... Those four carriers..." he said. "You shouldn't be in Elemontera anymore. It's not good for you."

I stopped, glancing at him over my shoulder, then I just kept going. When I looked back again, he was gone. Glad that everyone, including my parents, was still safe, I headed toward Victor's lab. I didn't know what the boss would think about my parents, or if he'd found out about their connection to Lily, but would he immediately assume I was a spy?

As far as I knew, no one was aware that I'd even seen my parents or Lily. And I had Jaiden on my side. He'd tell his father we'd only been captured by Sheridan and no one else. Unless of course the boss assumed I'd been a spy all along, even before Elemontera found me. That wouldn't be good for me, but I didn't want to think about that. If I could get myself into that lab and infect the system, nothing else would matter.

Chapter 15

As I entered the store, I reached with my air for Victor. There was only one mind in the lab, and I assumed it was him, so I ordered him to come out. A couple of moments later, the door opened and he walked outside, his eyes dazed, his white coat stained with green spots.

He turned to me, his face lighting up. "Oh, there you are. Come! We don't have much time."

"Um, I don't think that's a good idea. Maybe I should check in with my boss first. I mean..." I put up a show for the cameras that were all over the shop.

"Nonsense, dear. This can't wait." He went through the door, and I followed. Once we were in the lab, I checked the corners for cameras and couldn't find any. Victor stood in the middle of the room, blinking in confusion. Tightening my grip on his mind, I looked into his eyes.

"How do you know Jack Maiers?"

"We've been friends for a long, long time. Since he was in college, actually."

"Oh. Does he trust you?" Who would have thought the boss would actually have a real friend?

"Yes, of course." Victor smiled.

"Why don't you have better protection here? Elemontera's labs usually have guards or special alarms and devices?" I could still back down if there was something I didn't know about.

He waved his hand in dismissal. "This is my lab, not Elemontera's. Jack offered, but I don't want any strange men or devices around here. They affect my experiments. All my readings would be wrong with so much technology around." He went quiet, and I pushed my element a little harder to get him to continue. "I tried one of his energy detectors, and my velinioam burst through its glass. Chemicals, especially elemental chemicals, are a dangerous thing."

Velinioam? I'd never heard that term before, and I had absolutely no clue what it was. "Okay, so what are you working on? Something for Elemontera?"

"No, I don't work for Elemontera." His brow furrowed. "This is science. Elemontera is... corrupted by technology."

My lips parted in surprise, but I just nodded. This actually gave me another idea. "You don't like technology much, do you?" I asked.

"No. I told you, it affects my experiments too much."

I looked around at all the glasses, cups and containers. Some of them had a shimmering or glowy look, which meant they were all enhanced with elemental energy. No wonder they wouldn't work well with technology that had elemental energy in it too. "But if Elemontera were to forget about their technology, do you think it would be a better place?" My element was starting to get uneasy, wanting to squash Victor's mind, but I held it on a tight leash.

"Oh, yes." Victor's eyes sparkled.

The boss might trust this guy with dangerous biochemical weapons because Victor was good with it, but I wasn't quite sure his mind was intact after breathing in all these strange fluids. Actually, the smell around here was constantly bitter, and I couldn't quite pinpoint where it was coming from.

If Victor was so good, he'd be in the boss's lab. But he wasn't, and not only because he didn't want to be. Elemontera would always find a way to persuade someone when they had to, but Victor remained here. I wondered why. Maybe even the boss thought he was a dangerous man and was afraid for his precious lab. "Would you send something to Elemontera to help them with their technology problem? Something that could at once shut down all the technological devices, like elemental energy detectors?"

He scratched his chin. "I think I might have something for that." He turned around so quickly that I gasped, my control of my element wavering, but I managed to get back in control. Victor started picking up various liquids, wrinkling his nose and shaking his head. Finally, he picked up two tiny vials, one green and one yellow. "This!" he said triumphantly, nearly pushing the vials into my face. I jumped back, willing him to stay still.

"What is that?" I asked. "And please don't use any scientific terms."

"When these two are mixed, they explode, and the mist that rises after that has the power to corrupt every device enhanced with elemental magic. The particles in the mist attract elemental energy from the devices and bind it to itself, causing the device to malfunction."

Okay, that sounded fantastic. "Does it do anything to people?" If something could attract elemental particles, then I had to make sure it didn't suck out our elements too if it exploded nearby.

"Oh, no. That's not how it works. Human elements are too strong for this, but they could be affected a little." He put the vials down and rubbed his fingers together.

"Do you have a container that could keep those two liquids together without causing the explosion until it is opened?" Beads of sweat were starting to appear on my forehead as my element tugged and tugged, almost begging me to put the nice scientist out of his misery. Shaking the thought away, I focused on Victor.

He looked around the room. "Maybe. I can put it in a grenade, I suppose."

A slow smile crept upon my lips. "Do it."

If I activated the grenade, got to Elemontera and said to the boss that Victor had sent me, there'd be no way they could take the grenade from me anywhere else other than in the lab without risking every device in my vicinity.

Not that I had to tell them exactly what the thing would do. Killing me wouldn't help them, and I assumed I could mind-control the guards to let me through the main door because the energy levels would be high anyway and trigger the alarms thanks to these liquids. It wasn't a perfect and infallible plan, but what plan was?

I waited patiently as Victor ran around the small lab, opening hidden drawers in the wall. He took out a dark green grenade and opened it, making me flinch. He picked up the vials and spilled the contents into a small bag. Then he placed the bags inside the grenade. Even though I'd never seen a grenade up close, I suspected this wasn't anywhere near a regular one. But as long as it worked similarly, I hoped everything would be fine and that I wouldn't regret this.

A couple of moments later, Victor offered me the grenade. "It's done."

"How do I activate it?" I asked, carefully taking the grenade in my hand. It wasn't heavy, and I was afraid to even touch its surface too much.

"Haven't you ever seen one of these?" He laughed. "Pull out that ring and throw it."

"Right. But if I don't want to throw it immediately?" Using the grenade on the devices would be useless, because then I'd need a bunch of grenades and the lab would probably be sealed off by the time I got there.

He frowned, but I forced my element to get him to answer my question and not wonder why I'd want to do something like that. "Just press that thing." He pointed at the top of the grenade. "And don't move your finger until you want it to go boom!" Throwing his hands up, he grinned.

"Yeah, okay." That sounded pretty much normal. "Are there any special buttons you added to it or something? Can it be deactivated?"

"No, it can't. And there are no special buttons, unless you count the special trigger inside that can blow up the thing if I press a button." He moved toward his desk.

"No!" I yelled, stopping him with my air. "You won't press that button." I carefully snaked my element around the signals in his brain. "Look at me."

He turned around slowly, his eyes glazed. "You won't remember any of this. You'll only know that today you were working on a great new experiment that released a lot of fumes, and you got this amazing idea how to solve Elemontera's evil technology problem. Then you remembered a girl delivered you something and thought an agent could do it again for you. Elemontera would surely appreciate your precious gift. You wanted to get an agent here as soon as possible, so you sent out the fumes above the lab to create a shimmering as a signal. One of the agents came and you convinced her to come into your lab. Then you gave her the active grenade, instructing her to go to Elemontera and use it on the devices. Understood?"

"Yes." He bobbed his head, his eyes blank.

"Good. Now you'll pack your things, leave this lab, and go somewhere you've always wanted to go." I pulled my element back and ran for the door. Hoping the grenade wouldn't accidentally activate, I held it tightly in my hand as I passed next to the cameras in the store, because once Elemontera inspected the footage, they'd have to believe the grenade was already active.

After I was safely out, I put the grenade carefully into my pocket and turned into air. As I came closer to Elemontera, I stopped on one of the rooftops. Making sure I was out of sight, I pulled the ring, my finger pressing the top. The grenade didn't react in any way, and I wondered if the crazy scientist had done something wrong and the thing wasn't even active, but I wasn't about to try it out to check.

Keeping my hand low and hidden under my jacket, I strode down the street, careful not to brush against anything or bump into any people. My heart racing, I burst through the door of Elemontera's headquarters. The alarm immediately went off. My air shot out, going for the heads of the guards who were already drawing out their guns.

"Stay back!" I yelled. "I need to see the boss! Now!"

"What is that?" A guard's eyes went wide as he saw the grenade in my hand. "Get that out of here!"

"I can't let go of it!" I screamed. "Please! I have to get to the boss!" I didn't even know if the boss would be here, but I forced the guards to let me through. As I entered the elevator, I let panic show on my face. I thought about my parents getting hurt to force tears into my eyes. By the time the elevator opened, I was sure the whole building was in lockdown. More guards were waiting for me with their weapons raised, eyes wary. I lifted my free hand up.

"Please, don't shoot. If you do, I don't know what will happen!" I cried. "Please stay back. Does anyone know how to deactivate this thing?"

The guards just looked at each other. Finally one of them stepped forward and offered me a phone. I took it and pressed it to my ear.

"What's going on, agent?" the boss's icy voice rang through the line.

"I... that man... Victor... he... he... he gave me this," I said.

"Pull yourself together and speak."

"Victor Rice forced me to take this. Said it was a gift for you, and that you know about it. And as I held it in my hand, he just pulled that ring and... he said it would explode and destroy all evil technology in here. Can you please send someone to deactivate it? I really don't know

what else could be in this thing and I can't let go of it."
There was nowhere else he could send me except to the
lab. Nothing else could contain the spread of a disease or
whatever else could be put in such a thing. "Please, sir."

"Why shouldn't I just send you out with this? Save
my building?" he asked. "You're just one agent."

Damn it. "Because if you let me die, I'll make sure to
let go of this right here!" I squealed. There was silence on
the other end of the line.

"Your parents have had an interesting morning. I
wonder if what you have with you is in fact a gift from
them, and not from Victor," he said, his voice strained.

"What did you do to my parents?" I yelled, my grip
on the grenade tightening. There was no doubt he was
watching me through the cameras, so he'd better be careful
with this.

"Oh, I didn't do anything to them," he said. "But I
can't help but wonder... I've found out some interesting
things about your family."

"Look, sir, we don't have time for this. If you want
to talk, we can talk later, but now I really want this thing
deactivated. I don't want to die. Please!"

The guards around me were fidgeting, and they all
looked like they wanted nothing more than to bolt down
the hallway.

"Hold onto it for a little longer, will you? I will send
my men to take a look at the thing," the boss said.

"Okay." That wasn't exactly what I wanted, but I hoped they wouldn't try to deactivate the grenade here. That would be truly annoying. The line went dead and I handed the phone to the guard. A group of agents squeezed past me toward the door, eyeing me suspiciously. I was sure the agents were headed to Victor's lab to confirm my story.

Three men and two women arrived on the scene a couple of minutes later, led by Jaiden, whose eyes were filled with worry. I held onto the grenade, my fingers already feeling numb. Jaiden stepped aside, and the rest came to take a closer look at the grenade.

"Did the man who gave you this say anything about deactivation?" a brunette with green eyes asked.

I shook my head. "No. He just said it will go off! Can you do something?"

"I can't see anything like this." The dark-haired man frowned. "We don't know what's inside."

"Maybe we could do a scan," a short, bald man suggested.

"No, you can't! Victor said this thing doesn't work well with technology enhanced with elemental energy. Unless you can do it from afar somehow," I said.

"Well, we know it triggered elemental energy detectors, so it definitely has magic inside," the brunette said. "The agent is right; scanning it very closely could trigger it. The detectors can read the energy that is outside, but if we direct energy inside the thing, it might explode."

"Then what do we do?" a man with grayish hair asked.

"Take the agent to the lab with it," the woman said. "We can create a safe environment and see what we can do."

"Is our agent going to be in danger?" Jaiden asked, his eyes briefly meeting mine.

"No, she should be fine," the woman said. "Well, she might lose a couple of fingers, but... we'll try to make sure that doesn't happen."

"What?" I said in a high-pitched voice. "No! Take this away from me somehow. I'll throw it... I'll..."

"Whoa! Calm down. I was just talking about the worst-case scenario. We'll return you in one piece," the woman said calmly. "If you'd please follow me..."

She started down the hallway, and I went after her, followed by everyone's gaze. Jaiden just looked at me as I passed him by, and I could see the conflict in his eyes. Maybe he wanted to come with me, but he wasn't allowed to go inside the lab, even in a situation like this. Holding the grenade tightly in my grip, I fought the urge to smile to myself. I'd managed to get myself a ticket into the lab. Now the only problem was how to find the main computer and infect it. I was sure the lab had several rooms, and I prayed I'd end up in the right one.

Chapter 16

My nerves jittered as we stopped in front of the glass door, the alarm sounding as soon as we came closer.

"Josette, would you please tweak the detectors so they detect only elemental energy coming from a real element and not this damn thing, whatever it is?" the bald man said, covering his ears. "We'll go mad from all the alarms."

I'd been hoping they'd turn off the alarms, but there was no such luck. The brunette, Josette, merely pulled out a tablet and pressed a couple of buttons, and the alarm went silent. My bracelet started to burn on my arm, and I had a bad feeling someone had blocked my elements.

Something must have shown on my face, because Josette smiled at me. "We made sure your elements don't accidentally come out and cause the grenade to explode. I know this is a very scary and emotional situation for you."

"Yeah, thanks," I said, while all I wanted was to squeeze her brain with my element until it shriveled. Blinking, I tried to stay in control of myself. What I had to do was find a way to infect Elemontera's system, not fantasize about killing people. The door of the lab finally opened, and I was hit by a sweet, flowery scent. There was a long white hallway in front of me with numerous doors. The biggest door was at the end of it.

But as I looked to my left, my heart got stuck in my chest. A huge sheet of glass covered the whole wall, and from behind it people stared at me. There were six of them in a small room that only had cots on the floor and nothing else, and they were all dressed in white shirts and pants. A girl of my age splayed her fingers across the glass, and something about her gaze was unnerving.

"This way," Josette said sharply, and I realized I'd stopped walking.

"What is this?" I asked.

"Our volunteers for experiments," Josette said casually. "Don't mind them. Sometimes they get a bit moody."

I swallowed past the lump in my throat. *Volunteers.* Yeah, right. This building was full of *volunteers.* "What are you researching?"

"Something that will greatly help humanity," she said, narrowing her eyes. "Why?"

"I was just wondering. Talking helps me keep my mind off this thing in my hand, and... um, my mom is a scientist. She used to tell me about her experiments when I was little and..."

"Oh." Josette said flatly. "What was she researching?"

"Genetics, mostly." My mother had made sure she wasn't on the list of those to take credit for genetic manipulation, so I assumed not many people would associate her with that or know her for it.

"Uh-huh." Josette stopped in front of the door at the end of hallway and pressed her hand to the device next to it, and then looked into it, but the light still didn't go green. Finally, she punched in some numbers and pressed her bracelet against it, and only then did the door open. I'd have never gotten in here on my own.

As the door opened, we entered a room so vast I couldn't see where it ended. Tall shelves to my right reached the ceiling, filled with stacks of papers, books, and vials. To the left were the tables with microscopes and various devices, along with at least a dozen computers that looked nearly identical.

I felt a ball form in the pit of my stomach. If this was the room I was looking for, how would I find the main computer? What if they didn't have only one, but a bunch of smaller ones? I had a device that would work only once. How would I ever choose the right computer?

"Come here." Josette led me farther into the room, and I saw more computers. Great, fucking great.

Various scientists looked up at me briefly, but then quickly returned to whatever they were working on. I could see energy level detectors everywhere, and I wondered how that didn't affect their experiments when Victor claimed it was so harmful. Or maybe whatever the scientist were researching was different. I was escorted to what looked like a tall metal box that had a huge sheet of glass on one side.

"Get inside," Josette said, opening the metal door. I reluctantly obeyed and was surprised that I could still stand straight without hitting my head on anything. There was only enough room for one person. Josette shut the door.

My heart fluttering, I wondered if they'd just leave me in here with the grenade and wait for it to explode in my face. As the door was fitted tightly into place, I could no longer hear anything, just see what was going on. Maybe Noah had been right. Maybe this was the stupidest of all the stupid plans I'd had, but hey, I'd tried.

Trying to calm down both myself and my elements, which were constantly pushing against the bracelet, I watched the scientists through the glass as they rushed back and forth. One man, maybe five or so years older than me, with short, dark brown hair and dark brown eyes approached Josette, his mouth moving. Her brow was creased in worry, and then she shook her head.

I couldn't see much of the room from here, but I did see a woman with protective glasses and gloves who was examining something that looked terrifyingly similar to a human heart. Josette disappeared out of sight, and I thought she wouldn't be coming back, but she did, pushing a white device that looked like an incubator on wheels. She and the dark-haired man tinkered with it, doing some readings and comparing notes. I was getting itchy and tired, sweat dripping down my back. After what seemed like an eternity, the door of my box prison opened.

"I think we figured out how to deal with your little problem." Josette flashed me a smile. "Come out, but slowly. We don't want anything to explode."

I walked out on shaky legs and stared at the device. "Is someone having a baby or what?"

The man ran his hand over his face, and Josette rolled her eyes. "Of course not," she said. "You're going to put your hand with that thingy inside, and then we'll make sure you can let go of it nice and safely."

"Are you sure this is going to work? I mean, that thing looks just like a glass cage with holes. Won't something leak through the opening?"

"It's made to contain elemental energy, and if we're lucky, it will slow down the explosion for ten seconds, which will be enough for you to pull your hand out."

"Oh, nice," I said with excitement I didn't feel. Although I hoped that Victor hadn't been crazy enough to make something truly dangerous, and that the grenade only held inside what he'd told me. Even if it exploded in here, the only things that would be affected were the devices. But Josette and her friend didn't have to know that.

"Relax. We've done this before," the man said.

"Really?" I raised a questioning eyebrow at him.

"Nah," he said, his eyes gleaming. "But it will be fun to see what's inside that thing."

I wished I was as passionate about it as he was. "So what do I do? Do I just shove my hand inside...?"

Josette pressed a button, and all the holes closed, the glass starting to glow blue from the inside. "You'll see."

"Are you sure this isn't going to trigger whatever is inside?"

"Yeah. But it will trigger it only once you put your hand inside. Come on." She grabbed my hand with the grenade and pushed it against one of the holes. As soon as my hand made it through, the glowing in the device intensified.

"Um, guys?" I could feel the grenade heating in my hand, or was that the device?

"Just a second." Josette closely monitored the device. "Now!" I let go of the grenade, pulling my arm out, and Josette quickly closed the hole. We watched as the grenade floated, and then it burst apart, tiny pieces and mist flying in slow motion. A couple of moments later, the whole device was so full of white smoke that we couldn't see anything.

"That was amazing," the guy breathed, his eyes transfixed to the device.

"Yeah." I stretched my tingly fingers, shaking my hand. Now I had to figure out a way not to get kicked out of the lab too soon.

"I'll take this to Casper so he can take a look at it." Josette started wheeling the device away. "Pierce, you take care of the girl."

"Thanks for not letting me die!" I yelled after Josette, and turned to Pierce. "Can I go now?"

"No," he said. "There are some other things we need to be sure of. Come with me."

He led me to one of the tables in another part of the room. Then he picked up some kind of a scanner and turned toward me. "I have to make sure nothing dangerous remained on you, before you go out."

"Okay," I said, aware that he was actually checking for something else entirely. If they were at least a bit worried a residue of dangerous material could be found on me, they wouldn't have let me roam around without protection, and they wouldn't be just walking and talking with me. Something else was up; probably the boss's orders to check me for any devices.

I held my breath as Pierce brought the device close to me, moving it up and down around me. I prayed Lily's device in my skin was as undetectable as she thought, because otherwise I was screwed. Pierce frowned as he moved the unusually silent device, and I fought the urge to just punch him in the face and run. Would I even know if they detected something, or would they be the only ones to know and I'd find out when it was too late? The lack of noise from the device seriously worried me, because every damn device here usually beeped or wailed. Pierce made sure every inch of me was scanned, and then he set the device aside.

"Am I good to go?" I asked. "Or are we all going to die?" I watched his face for any clues, but he gave me nothing.

"We're not going to die." He placed his hand on my shoulder, watching me intently. "I just need some time until I get the results."

"Oh, okay," I sounded disappointed. "How are you going to get the results?"

"This device scanned everything it needed, and now the data is being analyzed by our computers."

"Your computers?"

"Yeah, the device automatically sends all the info to that computer over there." He pointed his finger across the room at one of the computers.

"Nice," I said. "And how long does that usually take?"

"A couple of minutes at most." He offered me a smile.

"So what are you doing here? I mean, what were you doing before I came in and disrupted your whole day?" I said in my sweetest voice, hoping I could get him to talk. I needed to get to that computer, but it wouldn't be easy to get the tiny device out of my arm without anyone noticing.

"You didn't disrupt anything. I was working on some stuff you agents found in Carter's old factory."

"Did you find anything?" I perked up. "We've been trying to get hold of those elementals for a while. It would be awesome if we could finally find out who they are."

"It's interesting, because we managed to get some DNA samples, but some of it was contaminated because the agents weren't careful enough at the scene. Some of it was salvageable, but it doesn't match anything. The tech team used the cops' and secret agencies' systems, and still couldn't find a match."

"How's that possible?" I feigned interest, leaning on the table.

"No idea." He shrugged. "Either they'd never been to the doctor's or never entered any of the systems. Or maybe they had someone delete all the records."

"But that would mean they had to have someone in a high position, right?"

"Or they mind-controlled someone who could do it. And of course now that person doesn't know a thing." He gritted his teeth.

"Are you... a regular elemental?" I wasn't quite sure how to ask without offending him, but if he thought that tainted elementals were a danger, then maybe he wouldn't be too upset.

"Yeah," he murmured, turning away from me.

"Do those tainted elementals scare you? I mean, I have two elements and I still get shivers when I think of what they could do to me." I twirled a strand of my hair around my finger, hoping I could get him to like me at least enough to show me something or get me closer to the computer.

"No, they don't." He eyed me carefully. "But their abilities... your abilities... are interesting to observe." He glanced at the tablet. "Your energy levels are very high despite the bracelet. Are you sure you're feeling okay?"

"Yeah, of course. I..." I looked away and spotted a camera hidden between the things on the shelf. "I just held a fucking grenade in my hand. I think anyone's elements would have spiked."

"Right. But I'm still going to ask your supervisors to increase the strength of your bracelet once you're out of here. We don't want any accidents," he said with a smile.

"What's she doing?" I pointed at the woman across the room who I'd seen holding the heart or whatever it was.

"Her job," Pierce said.

I raised my hands in the air. "Okay. Sorry. I know I'm asking things I shouldn't, but I'm a little shaken after what happened and I don't know what else to talk about. Do you have any hobbies, perhaps? Like playing video games or something?"

"You should just sit down here and wait. The results should be in soon."

It seemed like I would have a better chance of charming Josette than Pierce. Too bad I wasn't more likeable. Oh, well. "Can I sit over there?" I pointed at the area with the computers. "It's boring as hell here."

"You would only disturb the work of the scientists there, so stay here." He pulled out a stool from under the desk and placed it in front of me. "You can sit here."

I plopped onto it, fighting the urge to groan. Pierce picked up the tablet but didn't say anything, which either meant the results weren't through yet or they'd found something suspicious. If the guards even set foot in this place and came toward me, I was ready to use all of my energy to break through the bracelet and fight them, everything be damned.

"Looks like you're free to go," Pierce said a couple of minutes later, and I looked up at him in surprise.

"I am?"

"Yeah. You have to report to the boss immediately, though," he said, sounding a little sympathetic, or maybe I was imagining it.

I got to my feet. "Okay. Thanks."

"The exit is that way." Pierce pointed in the direction of the computers, where we'd come from.

"I remember." I turned on my heel and headed in that direction, but Pierce didn't follow me. I must have passed whatever test they'd had for me, and I was glad Lily's techs had known what they were doing. But now I needed to get to the computers because I'd never get another opportunity like this.

Looking to my right, I noticed a shelf with an empty jar on it, just as one of the scientists was about to pass by me. I moved out of his way a bit too fast and knocked down the jar, which broke into pieces. Tripping over it, I fell into the glass, which cut into my skin. As I was hunched over the glass, my hair covering me, I grabbed a piece of the glass and, gritting my teeth, sliced my skin close to where the device was supposed to be.

"Oh for the love of God!" I heard Josette's annoyed voice. "Somebody clean that up."

Someone helped me up. I looked at my arm as blood trickled down it and winced in pain.

"I'm sorry. I..." I said, but everyone just shot me an irritated look. Well, now they thought I was an incompetent fool. Maybe they weren't that far off. Anyway, if they tried to send me all the way to the infirmary, I'd be dripping blood all over their precious white floors.

"Come on." Josette grabbed my uninjured arm and dragged me toward the nearest chair, which happened to be right in front of a computer. "You're lucky there wasn't anything in that jar. You see? This is exactly why we don't let anyone in here." She shook her head as I sat down.

Since everyone was pretty much busy with other things, they didn't make a move toward me or toward the computers. They probably only used computers once in a while, and everything was automated, so no one had to sit there all the time. There was one woman at a computer just down from me, but she was staring intently at the screen.

"Try not to bleed all over the place," Josette said, her lip curled in disgust, and headed for one of the shelves. "I'll find some bandages."

As soon as she turned her back to me, I looked around for any cameras, spinning in my chair so the camera wouldn't be directly on me. Gathering my courage, my heart racing, I pushed and poked around the wound until I felt the device. Squeezing it out with a gush of blood, I thought I'd faint from all the blood and pain.

As I held the device in my bloody fingers, I waited for the opportunity to put it on a computer like Lily had instructed me. Trying to look as if I were getting really weak, I swayed toward the computer. When I waved my hand, my fingers collided with the computer's system box, the device pressing into it. It grew warm under my fingers, and I held it in place, hoping it was doing its job and that soon Lily would be able to breach Elemontera's systems.

"What are you doing?" Josette's voice rang behind my back and I jumped, the device slipping from underneath my fingers. Closing my eyes and wiping my shaky hand over my head, I held my breath.

"I told you not to get blood all over the place and look what you did!" Josette yelled, and I slowly turned toward her.

"Sorry, I got dizzy."

She huffed and roughly grabbed my injured arm, wrapping the bandages around it. "You didn't cut anything major, but I swear the cut looks deeper than when I first looked. You should really get yourself to the doctor. Now." She helped me up, or, rather, hauled me up.

I swayed on my feet and stepped on the device, kicking it farther under the table in hopes no one would see it or find it. Josette dragged me all the way to the door where a guard was waiting to escort me to the doctor. But before we passed through the glass door, I saw a man in white banging on the glass, his mouth open as if he were screaming in agony, his whole face red.

"You'd think elementals who pass the tests would be more competent," Josette muttered to the guard as she handed me over. As the guard helped me down the hallway, I glanced over my shoulder at Josette and saw her looking in the direction of the man who I'd seen, shaking her head in disappointment. I really hoped Lily would find a way to get rid of this organization forever.

Chapter 17

The boss paced up and down the office, his face pensive. As soon as the doctor had dealt with my wound, the guards had taken me to the boss, and I had to fight to stay on my feet because the whole thing had sucked my energy dry.

"Your parents have influential friends," he said finally, breaking the silence. "Did you know that?"

"No. I mean, I never really thought about it. They rarely introduced me to anyone." And that was actually the truth. I'd had no clue about my mom's best friend until she took me to Roivenna.

He waved his hand. "Yes, yes, because they were trying to hide your parentage, which obviously didn't work, but... I found something interesting in Sheridan's files. She thought you might be able to develop some interesting abilities. I must say I didn't really care who your father was, but now I see I should have paid more attention. Your energy levels seem high all the time lately, even with your bracelet on."

"Well, it's been a crazy couple of days, and my life was in danger at least twice." I didn't like where this was going. If he thought I could have abilities like Jaiden's, then both Jaiden and I were at risk.

"Yes, but I'm still intrigued," he said. "We'll try something new with your elements in the next few weeks."

"Um, yeah, sure." I hoped that by then Elemontera would be down for good, because I had no intention of doing more training or discovering what other methods the boss planned to use on me to get me to develop my abilities. A knock sounded on the door, and Jaiden entered the room, relief crossing his face when he saw me.

The boss sighed heavily, looking at Jaiden. "Is it done?"

Jaiden just nodded. I looked from one to the other in confusion.

"Good. You can go."

"What about her?" Jaiden asked.

"She'll come to you in a moment. Now go." The boss all but shooed him out of the room. With one look at me, Jaiden left me alone with his father again.

"You're not permitted to leave this building until I tell you," he said. "Your parents have decided to play a little game with me."

"Please don't hurt them!" I said, my eyes widening, my voice cracking a little. Lily had better be keeping her promise to look after my parents, because if this man came anywhere near them, I'd kill him.

"Make sure you don't ever cross me, and I won't." His smile was like icicles. "I'll send you some footage of them as soon as I have it, and I *will* have it."

I gulped, staring at my shoes.

"You can go now."

I strode to the door, glad that the boss hadn't suspected anything, but I didn't like that I wouldn't be able to leave the building. Still, if Lily's tech had gotten anything out of the computers, maybe they were already negotiating with the government. Well, *negotiating* was probably more like *blackmailing*, but whatever.

Jaiden waited for me in the hallway, jumping from foot to foot. He immediately pulled me into a hug, and I breathed in his scent, my shoulders relaxing.

"Are you okay?" he breathed.

"Still in one piece. But I lost my permission to get out of the building."

"What?" Jaiden gaped at me, then started for the door. "Let me talk to him. He can't..."

I grabbed him by the arm to stop him. "No. Don't. I don't want you to put my parents' lives in danger."

He lowered his chin to his chest, then looked up at me. "Are you hungry?"

"Famished," I said. Maybe we could find a way to talk in the lunchroom without being overheard. We just had to find a seat far from the guards and make sure the cameras couldn't read our lips.

After we grabbed some food, we settled at one of the tables in the back.

"What did you come to tell your father earlier? What is done?" I whispered, my sandwich raised in front of my lips.

"I was sent to deal with Victor, to eliminate him," he said, not looking at me, his lips barely moving.

"Did you?" I waited until his eyes met mine.

"I mind-controlled him to leave the city and never come anywhere near or try to contact my father." Jaiden picked at his fries.

"I assume Victor confirmed my story," I said, turning my head slightly away from the cameras.

Jaiden nodded. "I made sure he did. They sent me to interrogate him."

"I completed my mission," I said.

"Okay. Then we'll see what happens." He pressed his lips together, as if he didn't believe anything would happen.

I took a few bites of my food, and used another opportunity to speak. "You think the government won't cooperate."

"Something like that."

Another agent came to sit at the table across from us, so I didn't dare say anything else, and we ate our food in silence. No matter how hard I tried not to think about it, I couldn't help but wonder if Lily had even gotten any data. For all I knew, I'd connected the device wrongly or Lily's techs couldn't use it, or there was nothing useful on that computer. It did look like all the computers were connected, so maybe the virus would spread and infect all the devices.

"Moira!" Jaiden raised his voice, and I looked up at him. "Your arm."

I looked down at my arm that was wrapped in a bandage, noticing lines that looked like blue cracks on my skin that were spreading from the bandage. Calling down my element, the cracks disappeared. What the hell?

"Your elements should be blocked," he said. "How did you do that?"

"I don't know. I guess they're trying to fight their way out through my skin." I frowned. "Or maybe there was something in that jar, after all."

"I'll tell my father to unblock your bracelet, but let's get you to your room first." Jaiden stood up, offering me his hand, and I took it. My elements wanted out, and I wasn't sure how long I could contain them. Maybe the boss and the whole of Elemontera would finally realize that elements shouldn't be blocked; they should be unleashed.

Chapter 18

A week had gone by, and I'd been tasked with training Elemontera's four new recruits. My elements were still acting out, but my bracelet had been adjusted again, and training with the recruits and kicking their asses helped me to use up a little bit of that energy, which seemed to have no end. Just as I sent two fiery blasts, one blue, one red, toward one of the recruits, an alarm sounded in the building, but the sound was different. This time it was deeper and lasted longer. It wasn't merely a beeping sound; it was like a trumpet.

"Stay here," I said to the recruits, and went outside the training room. "What's going on?" I asked an agent who was passing by.

His face was white as a sheet. "We're in trouble. Elemontera has been surrounded by cops and a team of some people dressed in black. The boss is apparently negotiating with someone from the government."

"What?" I fought the urge to smile. We'd done it! Lily had managed to convince the government to shut down the organization, but why was there someone negotiating? That would mean the boss could get to live, or worse. I didn't want that to happen.

Running toward the elevator, I felt my elements surge in me again in a rush. As I got inside the elevator and pressed the button, I realized it wasn't working. Banging my fist into the metal door, I walked out. Why had they blocked the exits? Was it Elemontera or someone else? Maybe the other elevator wouldn't be locked down.

As I made my way down the long hallway, I ran into two guards who appeared to be ready for a fight, their weapons at their sides, helmets on their heads.

"You!" one of them said. "Get ready for a fight. The soldiers will be here any minute. Take down any of the attackers who come your way."

"Whoa! Wait, what? Fight? I heard there are cops and agents surrounding the building, but they're the government men. Why would we fight them?" I was hoping to confuse the guards and see whether they would really fight for Elemontera no matter what. It wasn't as if many in Elemontera liked the organization or lived for it. But, still, I knew some would agree to fight for Elemontera if they thought their families would be in danger otherwise.

"Because the boss is about to start a war with them," the guard said.

"Start a war? How?"

"We're going to blow up their precious agents before the negotiation ends." The guard smiled.

"Blow up? That's a terrible idea. The building could collapse with us inside." I frowned.

"No, dumbass. Not the building. Do you really think the streets around us aren't protected in case something like this happens? We can collapse the streets right under them and anyone stupid enough to stand with them."

"Okay. That sounds interesting, but then what? Are we going to defend our fort forever? Fly out? The government will send the army to our door. Or just drop a bomb on the whole building."

"We'll escape through the tunnels. Don't worry, girl. There's a whole plan for this, and you're going to see it. Just follow directions and try not to get lost, will ya?" The guard winked at me.

If these tunnels were on the maps, Lily would have to know about them. But what if she was just standing outside, waiting for whoever was negotiating, because the government wouldn't let her make another step on her own? What if the only thing she achieved was to cut some of Elemontera's financing sources? I was sure that if Elemontera simply moved into another building, they'd continue to be what they were. Someone would always be willing to pay for what they were trying to achieve. No, I couldn't let any of that happen.

Calling to my elements, I pushed them all into my bracelet, ignoring the burning sensation in my wrist. The bracelet flew off my arm, smoke rising from it. The guards pointed their weapons at me, but it was too late. I slipped into their minds, twisting the signals, and they both dropped to the ground.

Tapping their suits, I quickly found the devices that could start the elevator. As I ran past the training room, I stopped and went back in, hoping I wouldn't be too late if I picked up the recruits first. When the door opened, four panicked faces looked up at me. "Come with me. You're getting out of here."

"But what about our families?" a fifteen-year-old girl said in a shy voice. "I don't want them to die."

"They won't. I promise. Now come with me. We don't have much time." I sent fireballs at the cameras, knocking them to the ground. The recruits finally followed me and we all hurried to the elevator. As the door of the elevator closed, my hand hovered over the button for the floor where the boss's office was, but that would have to wait. I needed to get out first. Pressing the right button, I turned to the recruits. "Stay behind me."

"What about these?" The girl next to me shook her wrist with the bracelet.

"Fuck." I'd forgotten they had those too. But theirs were temporary, so they weren't as strong as mine had been. Checking if the device I'd stolen from the guard would unlock the bracelets, I finally realized there was no time and forced my elements into the bracelets, breaking them all. The door opened all too soon, but no one was looking our way because everyone was focused on the people standing outside the door. Before the guards could turn to see us, I knocked them out with my air.

"Careful," I said to the recruits and slowly opened the front door. Creating a shield of air just in case someone got trigger-happy, I walked toward the police cars.

"Moira!" I heard someone yell, but I couldn't see who. Noah and Lily came running toward me, dressed all in black, their weapons at their sides.

"Take the kids somewhere safe!" I yelled. "You have to get inside or get away from here. Now!"

"We can't," Lily said apologetically. "One of the conditions of our agreement with the government was to let them run things, and that includes letting someone talk to that asshole inside first. But I know we can fix that later." She gave me a meaningful look.

"Well, you'll have to violate that agreement. The boss isn't planning to negotiate. He can make all the streets around the building collapse, and he's planning to do that and then get away through some tunnels." The boss was probably only pretending to talk, because I doubted such powerful mechanisms could be started with just one press of a button.

"What fucking tunnels?" Lily gaped at me. "There's nothing in there! We checked!"

"Well, the guards believe there are some tunnels. But even if there aren't, they could use tainted elementals who think they don't have a choice to carry them somewhere. Hell, maybe they've even escaped already."

"No, they haven't," Noah said. "We're monitoring everything. We won't let them get away."

"Okay. Great. Then attack already!" I started toward the building, but Lily and Noah didn't move, so I turned to look at them. "Are you coming?"

"I'll have to ask the chief if we can attack." Lily grimaced.

"Who is he? Show him to me."

Lily cocked her head toward the man in front of the cars.

I let my element go for him, forcing him to act. "There. Problem solved." Turning on my heel, I broke into a run before anyone could ask anything.

Chapter 19

I threw the elevator key on the ground where Lily would see it and turned into air, looking for tiny holes that I could use to reach the floor I needed to go to. My search was successful, and I slid through an opening that led to the stairs I'd never seen anyone use before.

I flew up until I reached a door, but it was locked, and there wasn't any hole big enough for me to pass through. My anger rising, I materialized and slammed a fiery fist into the door until it gave. Kicking the door aside, I burst into the hallway, greeted by bullets. No one even hesitated, which meant they'd all been notified I was no longer on their side. Good.

Deflecting the bullets with my air, I elbowed the nearest guard in the face, hearing a satisfying crack of his nose. Dust flew through the hallway, getting into my eyes, and I squinted, a body slamming into me and bringing me to the ground. Someone was yelling to the others to block the elevator.

A waterball hit my face, making it impossible to breath, trying to choke me. I pushed my air out, the water bursting into millions of droplets, and I managed to shove aside whoever had pinned me. My anger was a hot living thing inside of me, and I let flames engulf my arms and legs.

When the air cleared, I saw one of the agents, a tainted elemental, like me. No, he wasn't like me, something inside of me was saying. He was weaker. Much, much weaker. With a smile spreading over my lips, I rushed the agent, trying to hit him with my fiery fist. But he enveloped his own hand in fire and caught my hand. Out of nowhere, sand hit my eyes and filled my mouth, sticking to my tongue. I coughed, my grip on my element weakening. Pain jolted through my leg and I fell to the ground. As I rolled around, I narrowly missed being hit by a fireball.

Spitting what was left of the sand from my mouth, I called for my air and reached into the mind of the agent who was attacking me. He resisted, but his face was contorted in pain. Before I could breach his defenses, a strong blast of wind sent me flying, breaking the contact. My head hit the wall, and black spots danced in my vision.

I saw Lily's men at the beginning of the hallway, trying to fight their way in with weapons and elements. I knew they'd be coming closer to me, and I had to get away from the fight if I didn't want to be caught in the middle of it. Turning into air, I dodged a few waterballs that weren't even aimed at me. Materializing in front of the agent who'd attacked me, I knocked him down, turned him and myself into air, and dropped him to the ground just around the corner. We had a minute or so until the fight reached us again, but first I wanted to take this one out by myself.

He regained his composure and immediately created a dusty cloud, but I wasn't about to let him blind me and escape, so I created more wind to clear out the dust, avoiding two fireballs aimed at my legs.

"You can't win this," I said, letting my air seep out of me not far from the ground so the agent wouldn't see it coming toward him. He didn't respond but instead surrounded himself with fire, which wrapped around his neck like a protective scarf. I realized he was thinking I'd try to choke him with my air.

A laugh bubbled up from my throat. "Really? That's all you've got?" I wasn't sure if I'd ever seen this agent before or if I'd worked with him sometime, and for some reason I didn't care. My air slithered across his fire and broke through it, trying to get inside his head. His dark eyes widened and his fire flickered in and out of existence, but my air finally slipped inside.

"Fight against Elemontera," I said, and let go of him, leaving him dazed. I ran down the hallway toward the boss's office. It was me who had to deal with him and not anyone else. That man had threatened my parents and hurt Jaiden more than he could possibly know. I wanted him to pay for everything. With his life. And I wouldn't let anyone stop me. Not even Jaiden.

A wall of ice waited for me in the middle of the hallway, and I hit it with a fireball, but it remained in place. Fuck! Increasing the strength of my fire, I let it surge out of my arms toward the wall until there was a hole large enough for me to pass through.

But after I got through, I was met with yet another icy wall. Whoever had made this would meet his end. I'd make sure of it. Something at the back of my mind nagged me to stop, to think about what I was doing, but the voice was soon drowned out by shouts from the guards. Melting the last of the icy walls, I turned into air, only a couple of feet away from the boss's office.

"There she is!" one of the guards yelled, pointing some kind of device at me. Were the silly little elementals trying to spot me with an energy level reader? How cute. I slammed into first one of them with my still invisible body, and rolled us both, so he would serve as my shield when I turned visible again. Bullets and elements slammed into the guard's back, who cried out, and almost fell on me. Creating a shield of air in front of me, I got to my feet, kicking the dead guard aside. I tilted my head toward the guards. "Get out of my way."

The guards didn't budge. Instead, one of them created his own shield of air around them.

"You think that's going to stop me?" I raised an eyebrow at them, and burst into laughter. They glanced at each other, and the shield wavered a little, but it held on. The other guard prepared for water attack, tiny waterballs appearing around him. The one who was holding up the shield lifted two guns and pointed them toward me. I sighed.

Increasing my air's energy, I let it slide up and down their shield, but without really touching it. They had to lose the shield if they wanted to attack me, and considering how red and strained the face of the guard who had put it up was becoming, he was about to drop it any moment. The other guy was surrounded by waterballs, but I could see the fear in his eyes.

My air waited patiently, and I waited with it. As the shield went down, I sent my air at the guards, slicing through their minds. They both dropped to the ground, the waterballs falling onto the floor in a big puddle. I sidestepped them and advanced toward the office. Kicking the door open, I braced myself for an attack, but nothing happened.

Peering inside the office, I spotted the body of a man in a suit lying face down on the floor in a puddle of blood. As I neared the desk, broken things crunched under my feet. No one else was there. The guy on the ground was too fat to be the boss. He'd escaped! That son of a bitch!

My element unleashed itself all over the room, creating a mini tornado that was ripping everything in its way and sending bits of furniture flying around me. Cracking my knuckles and taking steady breaths, I managed to pull my air back inside of me, but it still demanded of me to find the boss. Where could he have gone? I wouldn't be able to find any clues in this fucking mess.

Jumping over a broken chair that had landed right in front of the door, I headed back into the hallway. Now what? My elements wanted to be used, not wait until I caught up with the boss. I didn't even have to call my air because it came all on its own, reaching outside of me as sounds of fighting reached my ears, but there was no one in the hallway. No one to quench my element's thirst. Where could I find someone? *Someone meant to die*, my element purred inside of me.

A smile crept up my lips, and I turned into air, whizzing up and down the hallway until I found an exit. This time it was much easier to reach the forbidden hallway. I couldn't quite remember how I'd gotten there, but suddenly I was standing in front of the lab, the alarm wailing. Why did those damn detectors still work?

I sent fire at them until they started to melt, sparks flying around them and silencing them forever. The guards prepared to attack me, but I wasn't in the mood for a fight. My element broke through their elemental shields and I plowed inside their minds, dropping them all to the ground. Behind the glass door, Josette stared at me with panicked eyes, unmoving. I supposed she felt safe behind the door. We'd see just how much that stupid door could hold.

I stopped right in front of the door and placed my hands over the glass, unleashing my fire on it. But as soon as the fire reached its surface, I was thrown back, as if by some invisible force. Grinding my teeth together, I pushed myself up, dusting off my pants. Oh, now I was really, *really* pissed off.

Letting my air roam through the room, I looked for a crack—something big enough that my tiny shimmering thread could pass through so I could get into Josette's mind and force her to open the door. But there weren't any holes, so I sent my elements at the door to find a weak point that could help me crack it. But no matter how much I tried, nothing budged. I let out an angry roar, pacing in front of the glass like an animal in a cage. Josette just watched me, titling her head. What wouldn't she give right now to be able to run her tests on me, to turn me into one of her experiments?

I took a deep breath, pulling my elements back, unwilling to waste any more of my energy. Josette would have to come out eventually, and that thought made my stomach churn. The scientists had another way out of the lab, but I didn't know where that door was or how to get to it, and I couldn't be in two places at once. And yet, I couldn't let her escape. Would she stay here to observe me and take notes? I was just about to try another fire attack when everything went dark.

Only a moment later, red lights came on, and Josette's eyes were wide as she looked at something in the corner of the door. Something was wrong. She started running toward the end of the hallway, and I swore. I couldn't let her escape. What was it that had made her panic?

I placed my hands against the door, bracing myself for getting thrown across the hallway by some invisible force, but this time my fire heated the glass until it made a hole in it. I almost jumped up in triumph, but my head was starting to buzz, my vision going blurry. The door gave way and I pushed inside, barely seeing where I was going, led by the force of my element.

I stumbled through the door that led into the lab room, glad that it was open, and my element found Josette just at the end of the room. I willed her to stay still and dragged myself to where she was, my head pounding. I had to stop. I had to, but I couldn't.

"Please, don't!" Josette cried, huddling in the corner of the room, her eyes filled with tears.

"I'm sorry. I can't hear you. Did you say something?" I frowned at her. "Oh, no, you didn't. I only heard those locked-up people crying out for help, but no one came for them either."

"You don't understand," she said, hiccupping.

"You're right. I don't." My element caught her brain signals, breaking them in half. She convulsed on the floor, and I turned toward the next mind. The only thing I could tell was that it was a man, and my element took care of him. I was going through some rooms, or at least I thought

I was; everything was so hazy. My air never hesitated, not even when one of Lily's men poked his head into the lab. Someone screamed, telling everyone to go back, but his words were cut off. I finally slammed the door of the lab room, locking myself in.

Dropping against the wall, I hugged my knees to myself as my element raged around the room. "Stop," I pleaded, but it didn't want to.

Chapter 20

I didn't know how long I'd been sitting on the floor, holding onto myself, but my air was starting to throw things around, and when a bottle of some strange liquid spilled over, I knew that if I stayed in the lab, something even worse could happen. There could be an explosion if the wrong liquids mixed.

Slowly pushing myself to my feet, I tried once again to shove my element back inside of me, but none of it worked. I hoped whoever had tried to come near the lab had gone away when they saw what had happened to those unfortunate enough to meet my element. If they were smart, they'd seal off the whole hallway.

Cracking the door open, I peered outside. My element rushed down the hallway, but all it could do was bounce off the walls and carry papers and dust through the air. If I could get myself into one of those glass cells, maybe everything would be fine. Maybe I wouldn't hurt anyone ever again. But I didn't know if those rooms had been destroyed.

Bodies lay scattered on the floor as I neared the burned glass door, and I looked away, focusing on the rooms nearest to me. The glass of the cell that had been filled with people was broken, but the other one next to it was empty, the glass door intact and open. Entering the cell, I shut the door behind me. My element kept rushing around me, and cracks started showing on my skin, my fire pouring out of them.

I sat down on the floor, closing my eyes for a moment, and released my fire at the glass. Luckily for me, the protection on the glass still worked, and a thin layer of protection made my fire jump up and down the glass. Some of the fire flew back at me, hitting me in the face, but it only melted back inside of me. Not even my clothes or hair got burned. My elements knew me and I knew them, but something was very wrong. Why wouldn't they just go back where they belonged?

My whole body was heavy with exhaustion, but my elements didn't show any sign of letting up. One part of me wondered if I'd died and this was the hell the old books had been talking about. I banged my head against the wall lightly, wondering if maybe I should increase the strength of the elements rather than try to calm them down.

Pouring all of my energy into my elements, I pushed it all out, closing my eyes as the wind tore at my clothes and heat surrounded my whole body. A smell of something burning made me look at the floor, and I realized the cell hadn't been completely empty. A piece of cloth was devoured by my fire in a second, not even the ashes remaining.

The more I thought about it, the more I began to realize there was no way for me to stop what was happening to me. I knew elements could be spent if I used them too much, but mine didn't show any signs of slowing down. What if it took days, or even weeks, for my elements to completely drain? Maybe I couldn't even use them up completely because this space was too small for them. Maybe some of the energy just circled around and got back into me. But I couldn't risk going outside and hurting someone.

A strange beeping sound pierced the air, and I looked up in panic. The door of my cell was open and Jaiden stood in the doorway.

"No!" I yelled, getting to my feet and trying to push the door closed with my element, but my air didn't even dream about obeying me. Instead, it rushed straight for Jaiden's mind, and he immediately put up a shield of his own. My element hammered at it, trying to get inside. "You have to go. Please! I can't control this! I can't!"

"I'm not going anywhere," Jaiden said. "You have to relax."

"I'm trying, but it's not working. My elements... they're not mine anymore." I backed away as far as I could from him. Not that it seemed to make much difference for my elements. "I don't know what's wrong."

"They're still your elements, but you're not in control of them," Jaiden said, stepping inside. His face was strained, his shoulders tense. I could see it took him a lot of strength to make a single move and keep the shield up. I didn't want to think about what could happen if his shield dropped. If my elements proved stronger than his, I could kill him. I didn't want to find out if the elements I was born with were stronger than the ones created in a lab.

"I just want it to stop," I said, tears blurring my vision. "But I don't know what to do."

"Don't do anything. Just sit down and breathe."

"How is that going to help? And what are you doing here? You should get out before..." I let myself slide down the wall, taking deep breaths.

"Trust me. Everything is going to be okay. You have to think positively." He tried to take another step when one of my fireballs hit him straight into the stomach, sending him flying across the room. I covered my mouth with my hands, my heart thudding in my chest. Jaiden sat up, raising his hand as if he were trying to tame a wild animal.

"I'm fine. It's all fine." But his shield of air wavered, and my element intensified its assault, trying to wear down the shield where it was thinnest. Jaiden's arm turned into fire as he slammed his fist into my air, forcing it to back away.

"Jaiden, please. I don't want to hurt you. I'll never forgive myself if..."

"Hey, you're not going to hurt me," he said, getting to his feet and fighting to come closer. "What you're experiencing is just a chemical reaction. Your emotions and elements are heightened and I know you can't help it, but try thinking about something else. Anything else."

"All I can think about is that I killed all those people." I ran my hand over my face.

"No. Think about something that makes you happy."

My thoughts seemed to have scattered, and I couldn't recall a single happy memory. "It's not working. What did you say this was? A chemical reaction? To what?"

"When your bracelet was enhanced a few days ago, did you feel something like a prick on your skin? Maybe?" Jaiden was halfway to me, his shield shimmering so much that I was afraid it would burst. But I knew there was nothing I could say or do to make him leave.

"I don't know. Maybe. I can't remember..."

"Close your eyes. Try to remember. I know your mind must be hazy, but try to break through it."

"Okay." I did as told, blocking out everything that was happening around me until I could see the moment I was sitting on a mat in the training room.

A guard came to see me, carrying that black device that was used to tinker with my bracelet.

"I'll just adjust your bracelet a bit before you start training the recruits," he said. "The boss wants to make sure your elements can be blocked immediately in case you use them too much or lose control."

"But I'll be using my elements for the training. I don't think I'll have any trouble with my control." I gave him a hard look, unwilling to let him further strengthen my bracelet. *"And if I'm so bad with my elements, why are you allowing me to train the recruits? I could train by myself."* I crossed my arms.

The guard looked apologetic, his blue eyes softening. *"Look, I have my orders. There's nothing I can do about this, unless you want to speak to the boss first. But I don't think it would be wise to contradict him. It's just a small adjustment. You won't even feel it."*

"Okay, whatever." I rolled my eyes, extending my arm to him. He grasped my wrist with a tight grip, pressing the beeping device to my bracelet, a tiny prick of pain going through my wrist. Thinking how inept he was at this that he couldn't even use the device properly and was pressing the device too hard into the bracelet, I waited for him to be done.

"See? That wasn't so bad, was it?" He offered me a smile, relief flashing across his face. I pulled my hand back, rubbing my wrist, but there was nothing around the bracelet or at the spot where I'd felt the prick.

I opened my eyes and saw Jaiden only a few steps away from me. "I think something pricked me, but I couldn't see anything on my arm. Did they do something to me? Do you know why this is happening?" The look I gave him was so intense that my element got even stronger, trying to find a hole in his shield so it could reach his mind.

"Yeah, I know, because the same thing happened to me a long time ago." He gritted his teeth, reinforcing his shield. "My father tried to enhance your element, so he gave you a combination of some drugs to do it."

"But how?" I tried to direct my elements so they'd avoid Jaiden, but they still wouldn't listen to me.

"That prick you felt was a tiny needle. You couldn't have felt much or have any visible spots, but that thing did pierce your skin and released a tiny amount of a powerful drug."

"What kind of drug?"

"I'm not sure." He frowned. "I just know it's used to enhance elements. Since my father hadn't realized you already had the ability to kill like I did, I guess he tried to get you to develop that ability. He'd seen your energy levels go up, but he couldn't have known you were holding back, so he thought you needed a little push."

"Shit." Of course the crazy bastard would try to do something like that. "I think my mind is clearer right now. Do you think the drug will get out of my system?"

Jaiden pushed away my air again, crouching in front of me, but not touching me. Our elements collided between us, like two stone walls trying to push and destroy each other, without success. "You'll be fine. Just talk to me."

That wasn't exactly an answer to my question, but maybe talking to him was helping. At least I wasn't trying to murder anyone or trying to find someone to murder. "So this drug or whatever it is... your father used it on you?"

"Yeah, when I was younger. Thanks to his experiments, I had my elements much sooner than normal elementals or even tainted elementals. He tried this on me to enhance the strength of my elements. It looked like it hadn't worked, but a couple of days later, my elements burst out of me, and... I destroyed some things, but my elements weren't really enhanced because I didn't gain any new abilities. I don't know why. Maybe because I was too young, or maybe because my elements aren't as good as the elements of those who were born with them. But my father concluded the whole experiment was a failure, so I'm not sure if he changed the formula since then or if he tried it on someone else. I don't know why he'd even risk this with you."

"Maybe he thought that, since I was still in the building, he could control any weird outbursts." I looked at my elements that were still raging around the room and melting back through my skin. "Maybe he thought I was much less powerful than this. Maybe none of this would have happened if I hadn't decided to fight and use my elements today."

"He underestimated you. That's for sure." Jaiden's fingers hovered over mine, and I pulled back.

"I assume you didn't react like this to the drug. Maybe I'm allergic." I managed a small laugh.

"No, it wasn't like this, but it was scary. I was seven and I couldn't even control my elements properly, so..." He shook his head, the shield around him still holding on.

"You seem strong too. I mean, you're successfully fighting off this mess." I waved my hand, and fire rushed around my fingers.

"I managed to snatch another vial from father's secret stash of serum." He smiled. "I figured I'd need it."

"Thank God you did. So what am I supposed to do? Just wait this out?"

"Yeah. And you have to regain control of your mind and your elements, because they're not really alive. It's your subconscious controlling them."

"Ah, wonderful. My subconscious is a bitch." The fire surging from my left hand died out, and I lifted my hand up, looking at my fingers. "It looks like..."

Jaiden grabbed my hand, his shield wavering and finally dissolving. I gasped, trying to pull away from him, but I didn't have anywhere to go. My air shot for his head, but he fought it off with his own air, breaking through my shimmering thread every time it tried to jump at him. His fingers still warm in mine, he recreated a shield around himself, but this one was more elaborate and it followed every contour of his body rather than just looking like a protective bubble.

"What are you doing?" I asked, my eyes wide.

"Just relax." He pulled me into his arms so my head rested on his chest. "You never hurt me before and you're not going to hurt me now. Trust me and trust yourself."

I let myself relax against his strong body, even as my right hand kept turning into fire. My legs briefly went invisible and started to shimmer. My pulse sped up, and I looked up at Jaiden's dark eyes. "How did you even know I was here? Did you hear Lily's team yelling a warning? I wanted to..."

"Don't think about that. Not now. Just look at me."

I swallowed, hoping my mind wouldn't go back to a memory I didn't want to revisit. Voices could be heard from somewhere far, shouting something I couldn't understand. Bile rose in my throat. "Jaiden! They're coming back! If they get near here, I'll hurt them!"

"No, you won't." he said, his eyes alert, his whole body tense. Shit. He knew as well as I did that if those people came within the reach of my elements, I would attack them.

Jaiden's hand was on my cheek, his gaze intent. "No one is coming. Do you hear me? It's only two of us here. No one else."

I knew he was trying to distract me, but it wasn't working. "You have to warn them. You have to..."

Jaiden bent his head and pressed his mouth against mine, his tongue parting my lips. I leaned into him, savoring his taste. Something sharp bit into my arm, warm liquid trickling down my skin, but Jaiden was still kissing me, holding me tightly to him. I felt like I was floating, my eyelids heavy. I pulled back from him but all I could do was fall down. He was stroking my hair, and right before my eyes closed, I could see blood pooling on the floor under my arm.

Chapter 21

Bright light greeted me as I cracked my eyes open, which only increased the pain in my head. I was in a small room with white walls, and when I raised my arm, I saw it was wrapped in a bandage. Something rustled to my right, and I turned my head. My mom was getting up from a chair, her long curly blonde hair splayed around her shoulders, dark circles under her eyes. She was at my side in a second, her hand covering mine.

"Welcome back, honey," she said. "Your dad will be here in a second. He's just gone to get me some snacks."

"Oh. I guess we're not in Elemontera anymore, are we?" The last thing I remembered was me passing out... I looked down my body, realizing my elements were no longer all over the place, but they weren't being blocked either, as far as I could tell. In fact, they were inside of me just like they should be.

"You're okay. Lily's men found you on the floor, bleeding." She clenched and unclenched her hands, the lines around her eyes more prominent. "We transported you here, to another one of Lily's safe houses. The one that is closest to Elemontera's headquarters."

"Is Elemontera...?" With all the trouble with my elements, I hadn't even had the chance to think about how the others were doing, or if Lily's team and the cops had managed to subdue Elemontera's agents and guards.

"Elemontera no longer exists." A smile touched her lips. "It was a tough fight, yes. We lost some of our men, but in the end Lily's team took control of the building. All the world knows about this is that Elemontera was involved in illegal experiments."

"That's great." I swallowed, remembering I was responsible for the deaths of some members of Lily's team. "Um, did I hurt anyone else? When they found me... Were my elements... all over the place?"

"No, your elements were fine," she said. "They told me you'd lost control briefly, but I'm sure it was just temporary."

"I was drugged with something to enhance my elements, I guess. My elements went crazy. Did they tell you what I...?"

"Honey." My mom placed her hand on my cheek. "Whatever you did, it was the drug's fault, not yours. You know that, right?"

"Yeah." I wished the drug had made me forget what I'd done, but I still remembered my rage and my joy as I unleashed my elements on people, destroying everything in my path. "Where's Jaiden?"

"How should I know?" She curled her lip. "He and his father disappeared into thin air. Special forces are looking for them, and I hope they find them, because what they did..."

"No, Mom. Jaiden helped me. He was there with me. He..."

"He cut your arm, Moira. You could have bled to death!" She raised her voice, her eyes getting teary.

I was sure there was a good explanation for that. "Maybe he knew the drug wouldn't come out of my system otherwise."

"Honey." My mom licked her lips. "You're tired and confused. We'll talk about this once you're better."

"So what now? Elemontera is down? Did the building get destroyed?" If talking about Jaiden upset her, then I wouldn't talk about him.

"Most of the building is not functional anymore because it couldn't withstand all the fighting with elements and guns. But it's going to be renovated and turned into a safe place for tainted elementals. It will become an organization that will help them, not hunt them."

"Wait." I slowly pushed myself up, ignoring the pain. "A safe place for elementals like me? You're kidding, right?"

My mom looked away. "Lily made a deal with the government. They still don't want the public to know about tainted elementals. Well, let's just say they want rumors to stay rumors. And they want to know that they're safe from such elementals, so they'll let Lily run a new organization. She'll have to find tainted elementals and keep track of them to make sure no one does anything that could harm other people. If some of the elementals want to train or need a place to stay, she'll welcome them into the new headquarters."

"What?" I gaped at her. "They want to track us all down? And what? Put a chip in us like in some stray dogs so they can come pick us up if we make a wrong move? Or will the chip be able to kill us immediately? And who will get to decide this? Lily? And who will work for her to help her find those like me? Is it regular elementals, carriers, and element preservers? If yes, then I see a big problem in this nice new idea. How is that going to be different from Elemontera?"

"Some of Elemontera's agents have already agreed that they want to help. No one is going to get hurt. You can participate too, if you want. You've helped Lily and the others a lot. I'm sure she'll listen to what you have to say. Maybe the new organization does sound like Elemontera a little, but if we keep track of tainted elementals and make sure they don't misuse their abilities, then we might be able to officially reveal your existence to the public one day, and people will know that they're safe and don't have to worry. All Lily is trying to do is to make sure no one will want to harm tainted elements once the truth is out."

I rolled my eyes. "As if they'd ever catch us."

"Well, maybe they'd have trouble catching you, but if many people came together, I'm sure it wouldn't be so easy for anyone, even with mind control. And if they can't get to the elementals, they might even come for their families."

I didn't even want to consider that someone could attack my family simply because of what I was. "What about the experiments? Are those continuing too?"

"No, definitely not," she said adamantly. "What Elemontera was doing... it was horrible."

"Did you get my message and check what I asked you to?" I asked curiously.

"Yeah, Noah brought it to me. Didn't look too pleased about it." She gave me a disapproving look. "I think I figured out what was happening to those poor people. Elemontera was trying to change the genetic code of adults, similarly to what we did with fetuses, but it didn't work, because elements were already mature, not still in development like those of unborn babies."

"But it worked for some. I mean, I've seen one man use his new elements once." Right until Jaiden had shot him.

"It had to be only for a short time. All of these people died eventually, some sooner, some later, but none of them survived. Their bodies couldn't hold the elements, so they'd just... well, most died in pain and agony as their elements ripped their way out of their bodies." She grimaced. "As for that vial that you sent me, I'm afraid the sample was too small. I tried to recreate it, but it wasn't completely identical, so... Why did you want a permanent version of that serum? What does it do?" She arched her eyebrows.

"I was hoping it would help those people," I lied. My mom wouldn't be pleased that I was trying to find a permanent solution for Jaiden's problem with weakening elements.

"I doubt anything would help them. That kind of experimenting..." She shook her head. "I don't know why anyone would try something so horrible."

"I'm sure someone would pay good money for it, especially if there's even a slight chance of success."

"Jack Maiers must have shown his benefactors one of you and convinced them they could be like that. No one told them that you were born with those abilities."

"Jaiden wasn't born with them," I said, and my mom frowned.

"What do you mean?"

"He's like two years older than me. You came up with genetic manipulation after he was born."

"Then how is he still...?" Her eyes widened.

"His father experimented on him as a baby and was successful, but after that, he could never repeat it with someone older. And since it's adults who want enhanced elements and are willing to pay for it, he had to come up with something new, and that clearly didn't work."

My mom sighed. "Sounds intriguing, but Jaiden's case must have been an exception. We can't kill thousands of people to enable just a few to have more powerful elements. That would be absurd!"

I nodded. "We can't let those experiments happen ever again. What about that address? Did you check that out? I found it in Sheridan's office."

"Yeah." She glanced around uneasily. "It's an address of one of Marlau's houses. I don't think you should go anywhere near there. You've never been one of them."

"Um, okay." I briefly wondered who'd killed more people: my biological father or me. "I'll need you to run some tests on me."

"Why? The doctors already made sure everything was fine with you. We even checked your energy levels. It's all as it should be."

"I need to be sure, because I think my elements were out of control a bit even before the drug pushed them to their worst. There are things I've done that... I just want to make sure that it doesn't happen again." I didn't want my elements to control my life. Maybe Jaiden was right and the behavior of my elements was a product of my emotional state and subconscious, but I didn't want the part of me that enjoyed messing with people's minds to get the best of me.

"If it will put your mind at ease, I'll do whatever tests you want me to," she said, bending down and kissing my forehead. The door swung open and my dad burst inside, carrying a tray with food.

"Did you say you wanted more fries or more chicken? I totally…" his voice trailed off as his eyes fell on me. A smile broke out on his face, and he dumped the tray on a chair.

"I knew she'd wake up while I was fetching you food! God, woman, couldn't you have been hungry a couple of minutes earlier?" He glared at my mom, but he was smiling. Then he turned to me. "Hey, sweetie. How are you feeling?"

"Hungry," I said as he pulled me into his arms.

"Well, good thing that I brought food." He winked at me.

Chapter 22

As soon as I was able to get on my feet without help, I told my parents I needed to talk to Lily, and they'd taken me to a big office with an elegant dark blue table and matching chairs. Lily stood by the huge window, gazing at the city. Her black hair was tied in a braid, and her left arm was bandaged. A smile appeared on her lips when she turned toward me.

"Hello, Moira. Nice to see you up," she said.

"I heard some things about your deal with the government," I said carefully.

"You have nothing to worry about. Elementals like you will no longer be hunted." She came closer to the table, leaning on one of the chairs. "And no one will hold anyone anywhere against their will or do experiments."

"Sounds good, but I also heard you're going to be actively searching for tainted elementals and track them. That kind of concerns me." I crossed my arms.

"You do realize your abilities are very... special. Someone with that much power could do very bad things and we might not be able to even discover their identity. Elemontera was somewhat notorious for killing those who misused their abilities, so most of the elementals behaved. But we need to know exactly how many of you are out there, and we need to be able to catch those who are a danger for everyone."

"Are you talking about those like me?" I was well aware of the danger, but I didn't want people to judge all tainted elementals based on what a few of us had done or could do.

"You're not a danger for anyone. What happened with your elements wasn't your fault. You were a double agent, and we all know such missions have certain consequences. And thanks to you, the government gave me a chance to change things. But there are things that I had to agree to so they wouldn't put someone even worse than Jack Maiers in charge. We were lucky there was enough evidence against Elemontera, so the government didn't have a choice, but they're not exactly happy with this." She clasped her hands. "Still, I'm planning to run things my way, as always. You can ask your mother if you don't believe me, but we really are trying to do the right thing, even if that goes against the rules." She winked at me. "We just have to be careful."

Maybe she was right. Lily didn't seem like one of those people who'd issue a kill order for hundreds of innocent people out of fear, and she certainly had experience with oppressed groups, but she'd never be one of us. "My mom told me you were hiring tainted elementals to help you out. Did you get many applications?"

"Yeah, some ex-Elemontera agents would love to help out. What about you? You've done so much for us already, but I'm sure you'd be a great addition to our organization." She beamed.

"I don't know." I shrugged. "I could help out from time to time, I guess, but I don't want to be your full-time agent or anything."

She hesitated, looking at her hands.

"What is it?"

"Well, we have one problem, but I don't want to bother you. You've barely..."

"Just say it. You obviously need me to do something for you, so cut the crap and tell me." I tapped my foot against the floor.

"The thing is, I don't really trust any of our new agents with this. They've just been freed from Elemontera and I'm still not sure where their loyalties lie. You, on the other hand, I totally trust. Elemontera is gone, but the man behind it is still alive out there somewhere. I've sent my team to look for him, but we're not having much luck."

"You want me to help you catch him. But I don't know how. I'm not psychic. Besides, he's a regular elemental. All you need to do is track him down and get him." Just because I'd been training with Elemontera and somehow successfully fulfilled my mission didn't mean that

I was a secret agent. I had no clue how to find someone, unless they were shimmering.

"It's not that simple. He has a powerful guard, and that's where you come in. He wouldn't have escaped if his son hadn't helped him. So find Jaiden, and you'll find his father. All we need is both of them in custody. Although, if something happened to them on the way to prison, I wouldn't mind." She flashed me a smile. I must have looked as horrified as I felt, because her smile vanished. "You're not still into that boy, are you? He left you to bleed to death and escaped before anyone could catch him. He's killed way too many people, including the officer who went to negotiate with his father."

I just stared at her. This is exactly what I'd been afraid of. Lily might not hurt innocent people, but as soon as she thought someone was guilty of something, she was ready to gun them down. "I've been at the office. That man had been shot. I saw the blood. How can you know it was Jaiden who pulled the trigger?"

"He probably didn't pull the trigger, but someone did. Still, our investigators confirmed that the officer had died of a cardiac arrest and not the gun wound."

I wondered if she also had a list of people I'd killed, or if that had been all deleted because I was her agent and I'd helped her obtain what she wanted. "Does this mean all agents who've done bad things while working for Elemontera will end up in jail or something?"

"No, of course not. They didn't have a choice, but Jaiden did. He could have overpowered his father in the blink of an eye, but he didn't. After all, he's his father's son. If he were innocent, he wouldn't be protecting his father, he wouldn't have tried to kill you, and he wouldn't have run from us."

I had a very good idea why Jaiden was still protecting his father, but if I argued more in Jaiden's favor, Lily would never listen to me and she'd send someone else after him. I couldn't let that happen. "Right."

"So you'll do it? He's very strong, and I believe you're the only one who can match that."

"Yeah, I'll try, but I bet it won't be easy. They may have both already left the city. They could be anywhere by now."

"That's what I'm afraid of, but you might be able to extract information from people. Maybe someone has seen them."

"I'll see what I can do." Even if her intentions were good, I didn't know how the whole plan would unfold, so it was better for me to stick around.

"Oh, and report any tainted elementals you spot, or, even better, bring them here. We want to make sure everyone knows there's nothing to be afraid of. We're not Elemontera."

Maybe if she kept saying this to herself over and over again, she'd believe it. "What about those rogue elementals? While I was in Elemontera, I discovered they might be a part of some weird cult that believes one person will get all the elements and sub-elements. They left behind a whole bunch of old books about prophecies." If Lily wanted to find potentially dangerous elementals, she should focus on Raven and her group first.

"As far as I'm concerned, they were trying to bring down Elemontera. Now they no longer have an enemy. We will try to reach out to them, and I hope they won't give us trouble. Those books were probably some kind of a tactic or distraction until they found a way to attack. Maybe they just wanted to see how many of Elemontera's agents would come."

"I think we should keep an eye on them. Marissa saw some of them, so I suppose she gave you their descriptions. Did you find out who they are?"

"We tried, but no one really matches the description, or too many people do, and Marissa can't quite remember them, so let's just hope they'll reappear now that the air is clear," she said. "Oh, I almost forgot. Do you know your friends are here?"

"What?" I hadn't had a chance to ask about them, but I figured they'd be safe on Roivenna. "When did they come?"

"Earlier today. Noah went for them immediately after we were done with Elemontera. Kenna had to stay behind, I'm afraid, but I'm sure you'll find some time to stop by the island and free her."

"Yeah, sure." I started for the door and realized all I'd seen of this building, aside from my room and this office, were mostly empty hallways. "Where do I find the others?"

"Go to the end of the hallway. The elevator will take you to the second floor. You'll find them either in the biggest room or somewhere just around there. I gave each one of them their own room."

"Oh, okay."

"Your parents insisted that you go home with them, but if you want a room here, you can have it."

"Thanks." I gave her a smile and closed the door behind me.

Chapter 23

The elevator door opened and I found myself in a long hallway with pale yellow walls. A thick orange carpet covered the floor, and I padded toward the open door at the end. I peered around the door and saw Noah and the others sitting around a big table.

"Hey, guys," I said, and they all looked up at me.

"Moira!" Marissa's face brightened. Ashley and Sam inclined their heads at me and then went back to their card game. Noah watched me carefully, his smile wavering. I took a seat in an empty chair next to him.

"I think I owe you an apology," I said to Noah. "I shouldn't have mind-controlled you."

He looked away for a moment, then his blue eyes met mine. "I thought you trusted me. I wouldn't have revealed anything. You know that, right?"

I picked at my nails. "Yeah. I was just..."

"Look, you don't have to explain. I get it. You were under a lot of pressure and your elements were a bit unruly," he said. "So what was it that you wanted your mom to check so urgently?"

"It was a serum I stole from Elemontera. I thought it would help with something, but I was wrong." I said. He didn't have to know more than that. "What are you all planning to do now?"

"I'll stay and help Lily," Noah said. "I don't really have a family or a home to go to. This place seems perfect for me."

"I'm going to see my family." Marissa beamed. "They left the city a few months ago because they thought they'd never see me again, but now that they know I'm alive, they're coming back!"

"That's great." I offered her a smile.

"We're going to stay here until we find a place to live," Sam said, giving Ashley a loving look. My eyebrows shot upward. Many things must have happened while I was gone.

"What about you?" Noah asked, his eyes boring into mine. "Are you going back home with your parents? Back to college?"

"I haven't really thought about college at all," I said. "Lily has a mission for me that needs to be done, but yeah, I'll go home."

I didn't want to live in a place that reminded me so much of Elemontera. Actually, any building that wasn't my home and was full of agents and guards reminded me of Elemontera. My house wasn't that far away, and I was sure my parents would love me to live with them again. Going back to college would have to wait, though, because I needed some time to recover and think things through.

"Nick asked for a favor," Noah said. "He stayed with Kenna on Roivenna because she can't leave, but he hopes you can heal her brain like you healed his."

"Yeah, I'll do it in a few days. Just need to make sure I'm ready for something like that." I got to my feet. "Actually, I have to see my mom about something. See you all later."

Noah got up too. "I wanted to talk to you in private."

"Sure. Come on." We walked out of the room, and Noah stopped me when we were well out of earshot of the others.

"Lily wants you to find Jaiden and his father, doesn't she?" He regarded me carefully.

"Yeah, but I told her they're probably far away from here by now."

"How are you holding up? I mean, you trusted Jaiden and he almost killed you."

"Is that what Lily told you?"

His brows pulled in. "Yeah. Isn't that what happened?"

"Not quite," I said. "I think I would have hurt more people if he hadn't stopped me."

"You could have bled to death!" he snarled.

"No. He knew Lily's men were coming and that they'd take care of me." Noah had been Jaiden's friend once. Surely he'd understand that not all Jaiden's actions had been ill-intentioned.

"And that is why he just left and didn't even bother to check if you were fine?"

I sighed. "If he had stayed, they would have killed him." If Lily was ready to kill the boss, I had no doubt she'd do the same with Jaiden, especially after he'd helped his father. She'd wanted him out of the picture.

"Don't tell me you're excusing his behavior and everything that he's done!" Noah curled his lip.

"I'm not, but I do understand why he's done some of these things." I didn't want to tell anyone about Jaiden's expiring elements, because they'd surely try to use that against him, and yes, it did sound incredibly selfish that he'd obeyed his father's orders because he wanted to keep his elements, but things were rarely that simple. I wanted to give Jaiden a second chance, even if no one else did. But first I had to find him. I reached out and clapped Noah on the shoulder. "Is there anything else you wanted to talk to me about?"

"No, I..."

"Good. See you later." I waved at him and hurried to the elevator.

After my mom and the doctors had run all the tests they could on me for almost a week, they confirmed everything looked normal. I'd practiced enough with my elements to regain my confidence, so I turned into air and flew out of the building, rising above the city.

Everything looked so calm and peaceful, the morning sunshine still too weak to warm me. The sky was so incredibly blue that I almost wanted to surge up as far as possible. I headed out to the sea, flying lower so I could breathe in the amazing salty scent of the waves. Going back to Roivenna seemed so unreal that for a moment I thought I was dreaming, but as I knocked on the door of the hideout, I knew that it wasn't a dream.

"Moira!" Joy spread across Nick's face when he opened the door and let me pass through. He immediately pulled me into a tight hug.

"Hey," I said and saw Kenna standing behind him, chewing on her lip, her arms crossed. Her dark brown hair was even longer than it had been the last time I saw her, and her hazel eyes were wary.

"Are you sure she can help?" She gave her twin brother a skeptical look.

"I wouldn't be here with you now if she hadn't fixed the mind control," he said. "You're going to be okay. Moira knows what she's doing."

"I don't know about this." Kenna backed away from me. "I don't want to stay in here any longer, but I don't want to die either." She pinned me with a cold stare. "What if your control falters? Will I convulse on the floor and die?"

"Kenna!" Nick said, aghast.

"Well, she's a killer, Nick! Easy for you to say to trust her when she didn't have that damn ability when she was in your mind!" she yelled.

Nick went over to her, putting his arms around her. "Nothing bad will happen. If Moira feels something is wrong, she'll stop." His eyes darted to mine as if he were urging me to say something.

"I know you don't trust me, but I've been through every test possible, and I can assure you I'm fully in control of my elements." I said.

Kenna's eyes flitted from Nick to me. "Okay. I'll do it. But promise me one thing, brother." She gripped his shirt. "If she kills me, you'll kill her for it."

"Kenna!" Nick groaned.

"Promise me!" she screeched.

"It's okay," I said to Nick.

"Fine. I promise," Nick said grudgingly. Kenna finally let go of him and stepped in front of me.

"Okay, let's do this. I'm ready," she said, shaking her shoulders.

I called to my air and gently guided it out. The shimmering thread reached for Kenna's mind and she winced in pain, shutting her eyes. I could picture her brain signals, so I looked for the darkened ones and pushed my energy into them, reviving them. When everything looked fine, I carefully pulled back. Kenna opened her eyes and stared at me.

"Did it work?" she asked.

"I don't know. You should try it out," I said. She looked at Nick and turned into air, flying straight for the door.

"Thank you," Nick said. "I should probably..."

"Yeah, sure. Go after her. I'm glad I could help."

Flashing me a smile, Nick vanished through the door.

I stood in the empty room for a few moments, then headed toward Jaiden's old room, hoping Kenna hadn't destroyed everything in her rage. Maybe I'd find something in there that would help me find Jaiden. When I entered the room, I nearly stepped on a book. Kenna had pretty much taken out her anger and desperation on every item in the room, except for the computer, which was still on and recording the footage from the cameras outside.

As I picked up a few broken things, I wondered if there could actually be anything useful in here. I sat down on what was left of Jaiden's bed, pushing away the ripped blankets. The drawer of the nightstand was closed, so I pulled it open, but all I could find inside was a gun. I tapped the drawer for any hidden compartments, but didn't find anything.

Getting to my feet, I roamed around the room, but couldn't find anything that would give me a clue as to where Jaiden might have gone. I supposed the only option

I had left was to go back to the city and fly around until I finally spotted him. I didn't even want to think that he'd left the city forever. Although I could never blame him for it. He would be safer in another country, on another continent... so far away from me. God, I missed him so damn much. Pushing away those thoughts, I turned into air and whizzed out of the hideout.

Chapter 24

Three months later

Tired of yet another day of uselessly patrolling the city for tainted elementals or any sign of Jaiden, I found the nearest bar and ordered myself a nice cocktail. Glancing over my shoulder, I saw people dancing and having fun. Lucky them. I took another gulp of the strong liquid that burned its way down my throat.

"Easy with that. People might mistake you for an alcoholic," a voice said behind my back, and I spun around, my heart racing, my lips parting. Jaiden smiled at me, taking a seat at the bar next to me. He looked more handsome than ever, his dark brown eyes mischievous, his dark brown hair combed to the side. His black leather jacket tightened across his shoulders as he leaned his elbows on the bar.

I looked at my half-empty glass and then back at him. "Please tell me I'm not hallucinating."

His hand covered mine. "Is this real enough for you?"

I intertwined my fingers with his, squeezing lightly. "I thought I'd never see you again."

"I wouldn't have left without saying goodbye." He let go of me and turned to the bartender, ordering a drink. I pinched myself just in case. Nope, he hadn't disappeared.

"So where have you been?" I asked. He'd been eluding detection for three months.

"Here and there." He took a sip of his drink.

"Everyone is looking for you," I said, watching his face. "Because you helped your father escape, and because... they think you left me to die on the floor of that cell."

"I know. I didn't want to leave you there like that, but I knew they'd take care of you," he said, lowering his head. "It was better that I stayed away."

"And now? Don't you think I might try to arrest you?" I gave him a look from under my eyelashes. "I'm kind of working for Lily now. Maybe you shouldn't have come."

He gave me a lazy smile, tipping his glass toward me. "I figured I could take a risk in such a crowded place. If someone tried anything here, these people would be in for a nice surprise. I doubt Lily or anyone would want that."

I lifted my arm, pulling down the sleeve of my light blue shirt to show my scar. "So, should I thank you or punch you for leaving me with this?"

He grimaced, biting his lip. "I'm sorry, but I didn't know another way. There was no time to look for an antidote, and if those men came near you... The cut had to be deep enough so you'd lose consciousness and shut down your elements. Your energy was trying to keep you alive, so your elements had to be pulled back. Now, if you still want to punch me, I'll let you."

"Thank you for doing that. If I'd hurt anyone else..." I ran my hand through my hair and took a gulp of my drink. "Or if I'd hurt you..."

"You didn't," he said, his warm eyes framed by thick eyelashes.

"I assume you know where your father is," I said. "Lily is afraid he'll create a new Elemontera somewhere or continue his experiments. Please tell me you're considering turning him in and that you know where he is at all times."

He averted his gaze. "Don't worry about my father. I know everyone's looking for him, but I can't turn him in."

"Jaiden... I know he's your father despite everything he's done to you, but if you saved him only because of that serum... Maybe you should consider giving him up in exchange for your freedom. We could try to convince Lily to let you off the hook. At least then she wouldn't have an excuse to send a kill squad after you." Lily was always open to a good deal.

"I'm not ready to part with my elements. I'm sorry. Don't ask that of me. As long as my father is the only one who can make the serum, I have to protect him." An emotion flashed through his eyes. "That day Elemontera was attacked... I went to the office to find him, and there was a man pointing a gun at his head. That guy they supposedly sent to negotiate was actually there to kill him. Lily's men never intended to deal with Elemontera peacefully. And I just... I couldn't let that man kill my father, so I took him out. And it didn't feel like a wrong thing to do at all. But I do hate one thing about it, and that is that it never even occurred to me to just knock him out. I don't want my first instinct to be to kill people. Maybe Lily is right. Maybe I am a monster that should be stopped." He stared down into his glass.

"It's not too late to change things," I said. "You've helped elementals before. You could do it again. You could go somewhere far from here and start over. I'm sure there are organizations like Elemontera in other parts of the country, too. I think part of you did like it when you were taking care of everyone on Roivenna, and I know you didn't really want to go back to Elemontera, even when your elements were growing weaker."

He looked up at me, a sad smile on his face. "Your faith in me... it's a dangerous thing."

I shrugged. "Everyone should have someone who believes in them."

"Even when they don't deserve it?"

"Don't give me that 'I don't deserve it' crap," I said. "I really don't want to argue with you tonight."

A laugh escaped his lips. "Then what do you want to do?"

"I don't know. Something that we haven't done in, like, forever." I looked toward the dance floor. "I want to have fun. Forget that the rest of the world exists. Forget about our past." I lifted my glass toward him and then drained it in one swallow. He gulped down his drink too, and extended his hand toward me.

"Do you want to dance?" he asked, and I took his hand, hopping to my feet.

"I think my answer is quite obvious." I pulled him toward the dance floor, a smile creeping up my face. Tonight I no longer wanted to think about all the bad things that had happened since I discovered I had another element. For once, I could finally relax and not wonder if in the next second we'd get caught by some evil organization or by someone who intended to hurt those I loved. I prayed to God of Magic that nothing would ruin this night.

Pushing our way through the sweaty and drunk crowd, I swayed to the rhythm of the music, lifting my hands in the air and finally wrapping my arms around Jaiden's neck. His lips were so close to mine, and I looked into his eyes. Winding my fingers into his hair, I pulled him against me, our lips crushing together. When I broke away from him, we were totally breathless.

Closing my eyes, I let myself get lost in the music and twirled around, nearly bumping into some girl. Jaiden grabbed me from behind, his arms wrapping around me, his hot body pressing against me, his lips on my neck. Tilting my head, I covered his hands with mine, moving my hips against his. He let out a small groan and nibbled on my earlobe.

"If you keep doing that, I won't be able to stop," he breathed into my ear, and I pressed myself even closer to him, biting my lip. It was cute that he thought I'd want him to stop. But as I opened my eyes, I could see people glancing our way, and I tensed. Someone here could be a spy or tell Lily about this. Why did I ever think Jaiden and I would be able to have a calm night for ourselves?

"Let them stare," Jaiden said. "Or are you afraid everyone will know you are betraying your new boss? Kissing a wanted man? And enjoying the hell out of it?"

A shot of warmth spread through my body at his words. I tried to turn around to look at him, but his hands were firm on my waist, so I lifted my face toward his. "I don't care what they think, but if word of this gets to Lily…"

"Then let's make them forget we were ever here and find a better place." He dipped his head and planted a featherlike kiss on my collarbone. "No one will ever know you were with me."

"Okay." I found my air inside of me and let it out. Jaiden trailed a path of kisses down my neck, his hand slipping under my shirt, gliding over my stomach and raising goosebumps on my skin. Our elements roamed through the room, everything around us shimmering. We touched the minds of every person in the room, making them forget they'd ever seen us. That was so wrong, and yet it felt so right.

"Come on," Jaiden said. "I know a place where no one will bother us." I let him take my hand and we both turned into air, zooming through the air until the fresh night air hit us. We flew across the city, slipping through crevices fast enough so that no one could catch us.

Chapter 25

We materialized in the hallway of a five-star hotel, and I raised an eyebrow at Jaiden, who put his hands on my face and shoved me against the wall, his kiss almost bruising. Turning us both invisible, he took us into one of the rooms so fast that my head spun. When I was sure I wouldn't topple over, I gripped the collar of his jacket and pulled him closer until his mouth was on mine again.

He shrugged out of his jacket, then yanked my shirt over my head, tossing it to the floor. I grabbed a fistful of his shirt, almost ripping it off him. We kissed again as I fumbled with the zipper of his jeans, my shoulder colliding with the wall, but I didn't care about what I knew would be my newest scrape. When all the clothes were on the floor, I broke away from him and took a good, slow look.

"You're so fucking gorgeous," I said, biting my lower lip. Placing my hand on his strong chest, I let my fingers dance across his perfectly shaped abs.

He laughed, running his thumb over my lips. "And you're fucking perfect."

I opened my mouth, giving him a look through my eyelashes as I rolled my tongue around his finger. He stared at me, his lips parting slightly.

Only a second later, he turned us into air again. I found myself, visible again, on a big double bed covered with crimson satin sheets. Jaiden materialized on top of me, lowering his head so he could leave a trail of kisses down my stomach. A soft moan escaped my lips as a gentle breeze caressed my skin, making me shiver.

Jaiden's hot mouth closed over my breast, his hand caressing my inner thigh. I arched my back as he moved down my body, his tongue leaving a wet trail across my stomach, his element shimmering around me and slipping into all the right places. Nudging my legs apart, he looked up at me, his dark eyes filled with desire. When he placed his lips on me, I cried out, small hot shocks running down my body as his element and fingers teased me.

"Jaiden," I said, my voice husky. "Kiss me."

He moved up my body, his hands stroking and exploring. I wrapped my arms around him and slid my fingers through his hair, tugging at the soft strands. His tongue intertwined with mine, and the only thing I could focus on was the feel of his strong body. Calling to my air, I used it to flip Jaiden onto his back, and I rolled on top of him, pinning his wrists above his head. His dark eyes sparkled with surprise for a moment, but then he laughed, lifting his head to nip at my chin. I lowered myself down his body, flicking my tongue over his nipples. He let out a muffled groan, reaching out for me.

"Don't move," I ordered, intent on tasting every inch of his body. I loved the way his muscles flexed as he tried not to move his hips off the bed when I took him into my mouth.

"Moira." His eyes fluttered back in his head, my name a whisper on his lips. His body started to shimmer and his air spread over me, turning us both invisible and rolling me over so I was under him again. I gasped as we both materialized slowly, and I felt him and his element move deep inside of me.

The pressure inside of me kept building and building as he slammed his hips into mine, until a wave of warmth overwhelmed me, shattering me in pieces. My hands glided down his back, and I dug my nails into his ass as we both cried out in ecstasy.

I pulled him so close to me that I thought our bodies would melt. As I held him and caressed his hair, I knew that I didn't want to let go of him. Ever.

Chapter 26

I was in a room so bright that I could barely see the things around me. A silhouette of a man came into view, and I ran toward it.

"Hey!" I yelled, but the silhouette kept getting away from me. "Wait!"

My element shot out of me, reaching for the silhouette and forcing it to stop. When I came closer, I saw a face of an unfamiliar man, his dark eyes wide and empty.

"Who are you?" I asked. "What is this place?"

He lifted his arm and pointed a finger at me. "Murderer!" he cried, his face going blue as he convulsed at my feet. I turned around in panic and saw two more silhouettes coming toward me.

"What do you want?" I yelled, backing away, but suddenly there were at least a dozen people staring at me, reaching out for me.

The whispers of "murderer, murderer" resonated in my mind, and I covered my ears with my hands in a vain attempt to stop hearing them. This couldn't be real. No, it couldn't be. I was dreaming, wasn't I? But why couldn't I wake up then? The people were so close to me now, their pointed fingers brushing my clothes. I recognized the face of one of the men I'd killed in that alley when Elemontera had been investigating the rogue elementals' hideout. He stared at me, accusation plain in his eyes.

"You tried to kill me, you son of a bitch," I yelled at him. "You don't get to judge me for this." Or did this mean I was still blaming myself for what had happened? "Go away! All of you! Go!"

They didn't move, and I felt tears forming in my eyes.

"Stop yourself before it's too late," a voice said, but I couldn't see who had spoken. The familiar and unfamiliar faces stared at me, but their mouths weren't moving anymore.

"You are *the Murderer*. There's no going back now," another voice said, low and sinister. "You have been chosen."

"Moira! Hey!" Jaiden's voice broke through my nightmare, and I opened my eyes, seeing his worried face above me. I let him pull me into his arms, and I realized my cheeks were wet with tears. "Are you okay?" he asked.

"Yeah," I said, trying to catch my breath. "It was just a stupid nightmare."

"Do you have those often?" He rocked me in his arms, kissing the top of my head.

"Um, not really, but I think my share of bad dreams has increased in the last few months." I squirmed out of Jaiden's arms and sat up, looking around the room. Rays of sunshine were streaming through the window and falling on the pale cream walls decorated with golden patterns. A fancy golden chair stood in front of a dresser with a mirror. To my right was a nightstand on which stood an alarm clock. I gasped when I saw the time.

"Shit. It's 7 a.m. already. My parents are going to freak out," I said, trying to get out of the bed, but Jaiden grabbed my arm and pulled me back. Not that I had any intention of fighting him. I wanted nothing more than to stay in bed with him for hours. Maybe days. Oh, God.

"Why? Did they need you to do something for them?" he asked, and I shook my head at him. He was the only person who would assume my parents wanted something from me rather than that they were worried about me.

"No, but I've been kidnapped before and they'll freak out when they see I'm not home. I haven't left them a message or anything, so they'll assume the worst, of course. I don't want a search party looking for me. Where's my phone?" I spotted a heap of clothes on the floor at the other end of the room, but I didn't want to get up. My phone, which must have slipped out of my pants, was nestled in my shirt. "Shit." I let my element surge out of me, and I filled it with energy until it was strong enough to lift up the phone and toss it onto the bed.

"Nice." An amused look crossed Jaiden's face.

I quickly typed a message to my parents saying that I had some things to do and that I'd be seeing them for lunch.

"Are you going to tell them where you were?" he asked.

I tilted my head. "No, but I don't even know where we are. Last night everything was kind of blurry. You were flying too fast." I pulled the blanket over me and looked at him. "Whose room is this? If someone barges in on us, I swear I..."

"It's my room, so no one will be bothering us." He leaned forward and kissed my shoulder.

"You live in a hotel now? That's a terrible idea. They'll find you here."

"They will, but they won't catch me. Unless you help them." His dark eyes met mine, his face serious. I couldn't believe he was still thinking I'd do something like that.

"Jaiden, I'm not going to help them. I agreed to work for them just so I could stop them from finding you, but I still wish there was a way to get that warrant against you removed. I mean, I want to be able to go out with you without having to look over my shoulder and wonder if someone is going to see us and alert Lily."

"You still want me to betray my father," he said. "But even if I make a deal with Lily, I doubt she'll honor it. She'll just find another way to get rid of me. They all see me as a threat, and they're right." He looked away, biting his lip. "And your parents wouldn't want you to date someone like me anyway."

"Hey." I put my finger under his chin, forcing him to look up at me. "We'll find a way. Maybe there's someone my mom can consult so we can figure out what's in that serum and how to make it. I'll tell her it's for something else. I don't care if she and Dad don't want me to be with you. It's my choice and I do want to be with you, so they don't have a say in it." I smiled at him and pressed my lips against his. "And I know my parents. If I'm happy, then they'll be happy for me. But I can't tell them for now, okay? They could make things complicated. I'll need to find a way to explain it all to them first."

"I'm going to get you into trouble, aren't I?" He gave me a sad smile.

"You're not going to get me into trouble." I rolled my eyes. "Well, even if you do, it won't be anything I can't handle."

"Lily could be tracking your phone. Maybe she sent a team for us already," he said, but didn't look too concerned as he twirled a curl of my hair around his finger.

"She's trying to show that she trusts me, so she didn't put a chip in me or anything like that yet. But yeah, if she suspected I hadn't been at home all night, she could get the phone data, I guess." I groaned. "We should always find a different place to meet. That way they won't have it so easy when it comes to tracking us down. And I'll have to warn you about any patrols, although I think you've been good at avoiding them so far."

Jaiden's face was pensive for a moment. "I could get you one of those pagers that can't be traced. We could meet at a different bar each time."

A slow smile spread over my lips. "I like that idea. So where will our first real date be?"

"Wherever you want."

"How about that club near my university? Zero? Do you know it?"

"I do, but your university is like five minutes from your home. Why not some other place?" He eyed me suspiciously.

"No, it's perfect. The club is always full of students, whom by the way, we can totally mind-control, and Lily won't suspect anything if I'm so close to home. If she's not watching me or the location of my phone too carefully, she might not even notice that small distance between my home and the club. I can convince her I'm at home and even get there in time if I have to prove it."

Jaiden laughed. "She'd never dare attack us in a club. We could mind-control the people to shield us or even attack her back. She's not stupid enough to try that. That's why she did everything to convince you to go after me. She knows you're the only one who stands a chance against me."

"Yep, I can kick your ass anytime I want." I grinned, hitting him lightly on the arm. "But I really have to go now."

"One more minute. Please." Jaiden's arm snaked around me, and I leaned back into his embrace.

"You're going to say that every minute, aren't you?" I said. "And I won't be strong enough to tell you no."

"Okay, five more minutes and then I'm letting you go." He planted the gentlest of kisses on my neck. If I ever managed to walk out of this room, I'd call it an achievement.

Chapter 27

I turned into air and flew out of the hotel, keeping myself close enough to the ground so I wouldn't be spotted by any tainted elementals that could be nearby. But as I got into an alley, a shimmering cloud caught my eye. Materializing behind a trash container, I watched the cloud as it floated above the roof of one of the houses, not really going anywhere. Was it waiting for someone or simply observing?

I glanced behind me just in time to see another shimmering cloud heading straight for me. Turning invisible again, I flew up, hoping to avoid both of the clouds. But the cloud that was behind me caught up pretty quickly, and I rushed back down, hoping to lose it as I wove through the trees, houses and small openings. When I looked around me again, I couldn't see anyone, so I lowered myself to the ground in the backyard of one of the houses and dug out my phone.

"Hey," I said as soon as Lily answered. "I saw two tainted elementals, and I think they saw me too. One looked like it was about to attack me, but I'm not sure. Maybe they were just surprised to see me."

"Did they say anything?" Lily's voice was laced with concern.

"No," I said. "I'll text you the address so you can send someone to investigate. Or I could go after them myself. Maybe they're just some kids trying this out."

"No, don't go anywhere near them until we're sure they're not a threat," she said. "I'll send the team right away. You stay around in case your help is needed."

"Okay." I ended the call and texted the address. The elementals might not be dangerous, but there were two of them and I didn't know anything about them, so it was better that I didn't engage them. Slipping the phone back into my pocket, I turned on my heel and found myself face to face with Raven.

"Hello," she said, her blue eyes glistening, her long black hair flying around her. I reached for my elements, ready for a fight, but she raised her hands in the air. "I'm here to talk, not to fight."

"Was that you earlier? Following me?" I asked, but didn't for even a second think about relaxing around this girl.

"Yeah, it was me," she said. "I didn't mean to scare you."

"You didn't scare me," I said coldly. "So what did you want to talk about?"

"Elemontera is gone, and I heard you had a role in taking it down, so I wanted to thank you. In the name of my whole group," she said, and I glared at her.

"Was that why you were trying to sneak up on me? To thank me?" I raised a questioning eyebrow.

"I'm sorry about that. I wasn't sure it was you. I only recognized you when you turned visible again."

"Okay. Um, so does that mean you no longer want to kill me or anyone who used to work for Elemontera?"

"No, I don't want to kill anyone." She shook her head. "I'm just glad Elemontera is gone."

"Me too," I said. "I'm curious about one thing, though. Why was your little group stealing all those old books about prophecies? Elemontera thought it was some kind of a message, but unfortunately no one ever got it." I chuckled. "Do you believe in any of that or was it all just a part of some plan?"

She tilted her head at me. "It wasn't really a message. But prophecies are interesting, don't you think? They sounds very unrealistic and unlikely to happen, but don't you wonder sometimes what would happen if it were all true?"

"Honestly, I don't really care much about those things."

"Maybe you should," she said.

"What's that supposed to mean?" I wondered if she'd be able to fight me off if I tried to get inside of her head, because as far as I could remember she did have the ability to use mind control. But I definitely didn't want to piss her off. If there was even a slight chance she had the ability to kill and believed in crazy prophecies, I had to make sure Lily could track her down.

"You don't have to get upset." She smirked. "I'm just saying... sometimes incredible things happen."

"Look, now that Elemontera is gone and no one is hunting those like us, we have this center for people like us... a safe place. The woman who's in charge, Lily, is a good person, and she's making sure that everyone can live in peace," I said. "You could come in sometime. Find out more about those like us. If you're interested in prophecies, maybe you'd like to know more about our own kind first."

"Oh. You mean new Elemontera? You want me to go there and talk to your boss so she can... do what, exactly, with me?" She arched an eyebrow at me.

I licked my dry lips. "We're all trying to start over, so whatever you've done when you attacked Elemontera, we know you were fighting for your life and your safety, so no one will prosecute you for that. But if we all truly want to live in peace, we have to make sure everyone follows some rules."

She gave me a skeptical look. "Rules? What rules?"

"None of us should harm any other human being or use their abilities for illegal purposes."

"And how exactly do you plan to ensure that? With the help of a special police force?" Her eyes sparkled with amusement.

"I'm sure Lily can explain all of this to you if you would just come to meet her," I said, trying to sound friendly, though I was still ready to attack if Raven made a single wrong step. "If you're afraid, you can meet her in a public place somewhere. I'm sure she wouldn't mind."

"Okay, I might think about that. Who is this Lily anyway? One of us?" Her gaze briefly flickered to something behind my back, and I immediately turned around but couldn't see anything.

"She's not one of us..." I started to say and noticed Raven was trying her best to give me a fake curious look, the corners of her lips slightly upturned. She didn't really seem interested in anything I had to say, so why the hell was she asking? Was she trying to be polite or thought I'd attack her if she tried to leave? But she didn't look distressed. It was almost as if she was happy... as if she had me exactly where she wanted me.

"Yes?" she said, and I shoved her away from me, sending her sprawling to the ground. She was stalling. I didn't know why, and I didn't want to stick around and wait to find out. Calling to my element, I started to turn into air, but pain shot through my head like lightning, and I fell to my knees. I tried to fight off the element that was weaseling its way into my head, but no matter how hard I pushed, it wouldn't get out. Footsteps echoed behind my back, getting closer and closer.

"Get up," a deep male voice said, and I rose to my feet without even having to think about it. "Turn around."

I came face to face with a guy my age, with spiky black hair and piercing light blue eyes. Raven stood at his side, a smug smile spreading over her lips. The pain in my head intensified, and I tried to spot the shimmering thread, but I couldn't see it. Gathering all of my strength, I attempted to shove the intruder out of my mind once again, but it didn't work.

I couldn't even move or take a step in the guy's direction. My heartbeat racing, I called to my elements in hopes of reaching out with my own element and maybe getting Raven to at least break the guy's concentration, but my elements didn't even stir inside of me.

"We think you're going to be a great addition to our little group," the guy said, his gaze traveling my body. "I must say I was pleased that you passed the test. You killed those four men with your element, without hesitation. That was absolutely exquisite. We need someone exactly like you."

Shit. So the whole thing had indeed been a set-up; some kind of a test so the elementals could see if I truly had the ability to kill.

"I know you have a lot of questions," the guy said. "But we'll explain everything to you eventually. You don't need to fight me. You're safe with us. Don't be afraid."

And just like that, the tension left my shoulders, and I just stared at him, the throbbing in my head growing distant.

The guy looked at Raven. "Maybe we should find a safer place to chat. Someone could see us here."

"Yeah." She nodded, giving him a smile, but there was something else in her eyes that I couldn't quite identify.

The guy's eyes met mine. "We'll deal with your memories later. For now, there's only one thing you need to know about yourself. You've been in an accident and your memories are a bit hazy, but you do know this. My name is Blake. You're my girlfriend. You love me and you'd do anything for me."

I blinked, rubbing the spot on my head that seemed to hurt the most.

"What's wrong, love? Are you feeling all right?" my boyfriend asked, his eyebrows drawn together in concern.

"Yeah, I'm just... a bit confused," I admitted. That stupid accident had probably left me with a nasty bump on my head. Blake put his arm around me and we started walking down the street. "Where are we going?" I asked.

"Home."

###

TAINTED ELEMENTS SERIES
DIFFERENT
INVISIBLE
MONSTER

Also by Alycia Linwood

HUMAN

ELEMENT PRESERVERS SERIES

DANGEROUS
RUNAWAY
DIVIDED
NO ONE
RESTLESS
INDESTRUCTIBLE

More information:
www.alycialinwood.weebly.com

CPSIA information can be obtained at www.ICGtesting.com
Printed in the USA
LVOW07s1617040515

437168LV00001B/98/P